I Am a
Cloud,
I can Blow
Anywhere

EGMONT

We bring stories to life

First published 2007 by Egmont UK Limited
239 Kensington High Street
London W8 6SA

Text copyright © 2007 Jonathan and Shirley Tulloch
Cover typography copyright © 2007 Dan Bramall
Cover photography copyright © 2007 Getty Images

The moral rights of the authors have been asserted

ISBN 978 1 4052 2325 6
ISBN 1 4052 2325 1

1 3 5 7 9 10 8 6 4 2

A CIP catalogue record for this title is available from the British Library

Printed and bound in Great Britain by the CPI Group

Jonathan and Shirley Tulloch

I Am a Cloud, I can Blow Anywhere

EGMONT

To Aidan and his cousins: Shane, Miranda, Helena, Joseph, Aelred, Freyja and Anselm.

With special thanks to: Bernard, Agnes, Tutu and Musa Manyena, Edson Munsaka, and Cally Poplak.

CONTENTS

PART ONE: *I AM A CLOUD* . . .

THE NIGHT MARAUDERS

'Mulumbe, Mulumbe,' someone was calling me in my sleep. 'Mulumbe, Mulumbe.' The call became a cry. 'Mulumbe, wake up!' Curling into a ball I tried to shrug off whoever it was jolting me from my delicious rest. But the voice would not stop. It grew more insistent. It began to shout. 'Mulumbe, you must wake up now!'

I opened my eyes. Grandmother was leaning over me. She was shaking my shoulder. 'They are coming,' she said.

I could hear the terror in her voice. There was no need for any questions. I got up and followed her outside.

'Quick, child,' she urged.

'What about the others, Grandmother?'

'I will wake the others. Run, before it's too late!'

It was still dark and the earth was cold beneath my bare feet. Dressed only in my T-shirt and skirt, I shivered. Quickly the rest of the family emerged from their huts and Grandmother shepherded them into the forest. All at once the night was filled with shouts and screams. *They* had come.

It was mayhem, as though the whole village had become one of the ants' nests that my little brothers liked to poke with sticks. People scattered in all directions. Bumping into one another, they plunged shrieking into the trees.

At that moment a hand grasped mine. 'Mulumbe, what are you still doing here?' Grandmother half-screamed.

'Are all the others safe?' I asked.

'Yes, but now *you* are going to be caught.'

We ran blindly, lunging through the thick, thorny trees. Barbs lacerated my T-shirt and arms, and tugged at my hair like talons grappling to stop us. Crashing through the bush like warthogs, we thought only of escape. The smell of burning fouled the air. *They* were setting alight to the thatch of our huts. Over our shoulders the lurid light of flames leapt.

On and on we ran, wildly, not daring to rest. But the angry shouting of the marauders did not get any quieter. In fact all at once our pursuers seemed to be surrounding us. We both stopped at the same time. 'Grandmother,' I whispered, 'I think they are following us.'

She pressed a finger across my lips. 'Not a sound.'

Dropping to our hands and knees we began to crawl. The moon cast everything into silver shadows. How many times on other nights had I gazed up, entranced by the smile of the moon-woman? But now this same smile threatened to show us to our enemy.

We moved as silently as leopards, although we were the ones being hunted. I did not even make a noise as I usually did to scare away snakes.

Still the shouting and curses reverberated all around us. Sometimes voices came shockingly near, ringing clearly in the silver-coated darkness. Then we would freeze and wait, curled as small as we could behind a tree or in a bush. Once the men came so close that I could smell them: a harsh stink of rancid beer and hate. I had to force the bile back down my throat. Any moment I expected the marauders to come raging through the trees, charging like rhinoceros, knocking us over and grinding us down into the earth.

That is how I always thought of them: as an enraged rhinoceros.

They came to our village for the first time two years ago and took away my mother. They dragged her screaming into the night. I never saw her again. My father lost an eye trying to stop them. Anger had made their heads seem heavy and blunt, just like a rhino's. And they wore their hatred of us like a horn.

Silently, fearfully we continued to edge through the bush – an old woman and a girl pursued by a pack of marauding men. 'Keep on going, child,' Grandmother murmured. 'Keep on going.' She was trying to disguise the worst of the terror in her voice, but we both knew what would happen if we were caught. A rat crossed our path. I shuddered but did not stop. Far rather a rat than one of the men; far rather a thousand rats. In the darkness the forest seethed with a hundred unknown sounds. Tonight I feared none of them. I yearned only to escape the men.

We were deep in the forest when Grandmother suddenly stopped. My heart beat like a little bula bird held in a pair of hands. 'What is it, Grandmother?'

'Shh, child. I am listening.'

For a long, long time she stood there frozen in moonlight, still as one of the trees. I listened with every fibre of my being too, but could not hear any sign of our pursuers. At last there was a gentle finger on my cheek. 'We are safe, Mulumbe. For now, this time.'

Relief surged through me like a torrent coursing down the dry streambed in the rainy season.

Taking my hand Grandmother set off again. *They* would be gone by the time we returned to our village. *They* never stayed long. But just to make sure we did not meet them on the way, Grandmother took us by a path only she knew.

Now that we were safe the smile of the moon-woman became beautiful again. The stars glittered like her polished beads. As always the frogs called loudly, pulsing rhythmically like the lungs of the night. This familiar sound began to soothe me like my mother's lullabies once had, when all of a sudden a fresh terror tore away this new-found peace. 'Grandmother, what about Tom?'

A few days ago, Tom, my eldest brother, had gone with some of the other boys to graze their goat flocks in the hills. What if they had been on their way home and the night marauders had seen the light of their cooking fires? 'Grandmother,' I repeated, 'will Tom be all right?'

Grandmother did not reply. As we walked along, fear for my brother pursued me as terribly as the men had.

At last day began to break. One by one the night frogs fell silent and the first arm of the sun, stretching itself awake in the branches of the mopane trees above us, lifted darkness from the shoulders of the world.

The hornbills woke and began their noisy chatter. The sunbirds started singing sweetly. A flock of bee-eaters flashed by like a dream of colour. After the scenes of the night, and my worries for Tom, it was almost too beautiful.

'Mulumbe, let us rest for a while,' said Grandmother.

I sat on a fallen log and although I felt the sun warming my face, the chill on my spirits did not lift. 'Why do they want to hurt us, Grandmother?' I asked.

The old woman shrugged. 'Why does Crocodile want to catch Hare?'

'Is that a riddle?' I asked, for we often played games of riddles together.

'No, Mulumbe. It is the answer to your question. What else can Crocodile do with his sharp teeth? He *must* bite. That is his nature.'

Grandmother had a way of talking that made you want to listen forever, even when she spoke of frightening things. It was as though her words were pictures. But still my fears stalked me. 'Grandmother, is Tom all right?'

She narrowed her eyes and the wrinkles on her forehead deepened. As though she was trying to see something very far away, her eyes grew narrower and narrower until at last they closed. When she opened them again, she was smiling. 'Child, your brother will be all right. Now sit down here like a butterfly on the *munimbwa* blossom whilst I get some plants to soothe your cuts. Look how the thorn trees have hurt your arms.'

I had not felt any pain in the heat of our escape but now the criss-cross cuts began to sting. Yet despite this I found myself beginning to laugh. Grandmother had said

Tom was safe. Grandmother was always right. I watched her as she collected the leaves, rubbed them together in her hands then laid them on my arms. The burning eased to a gentle cool. 'What are you grinning at child?' she asked.

'The butterfly must open her wings when the sun shines!' I replied.

Both laughing, we set off again. It was my favourite time of day. Dawn had fully broken and the sun poured like honey through the canopy of the forest. The air was sweet and the ground, beaded with dewdrops, was pleasant beneath the feet. Later it would be so scorching that as you walked on it you would have to dance like a civet cat held by its tail.

As we passed beneath the mopane trees, the hornbills stopped their bickering and, laying their heads on one side, watched us: eyes beady, huge beaks roving. Of all the birds in the bush Hornbill is the most intelligent. In fact, of all the forest creatures only Hare is wilier. I was just about to ask Grandmother to tell me one of her stories about Hornbill or Hare when something in her face made me fall silent. There was worry in her eyes. Just for an instant, before she realised I was looking, her features were as rigid as the black stone figures my father once carved. Was she really so sure about Tom, or was she trying to protect me from a bitter truth?

Dread came over me. I would rather die myself than lose my big brother.

SEARCHING THE STARS

Devastation greeted us on our return to the village. Most of the huts had been burnt down, the animals and hens taken, our *ntombo* granary barns emptied. A deathly silence drifted on the smoke of the still-smouldering roofs. Grandmother's shoulders drooped at the sight.

'Grandmother,' I whispered, 'where is everyone?'

The old woman did not reply.

At last we saw a girl moving through the wreckage. 'Magoyela!' I called.

'Mulumbe, is that you?'

She sprinted over and threw her arms around me. Magoyela was my half-sister, the daughter of my father's second wife. The sight and feel of her filled me with joy.

'Oh, Mulumbe,' she said. 'We thought they had taken you.'

Although only two years younger, Magoyela looked up to me as though I was a grownup.

'Magoyela, my sister, where is Tom?'

'Mulumbe, my sister,' she replied, 'we have not seen him.'

Just then the air was filled with the laughter and happy shrieks of very young children: the rest of my half-brothers and sisters were emerging from behind a smouldering hut. They ran to Grandmother, their voices piping like wild dog's pups welcoming home the adults after a successful hunt. They were all safe. The girls: Buumi and Luuwo; the boys: Simonje and Namaanza. Only Tom was unaccounted for.

'Where is that lazy girl?' A voice harsh as the cry of the grey go-away bird cut through the children's noisy greetings. 'Magoyela, where are you?' It was Stepmother, my father's youngest wife. 'You are supposed to be looking after the cooking pot! Is it not enough for you that they burn our homes but now you must burn our food? Ah! Where is my stick? Come here! When I catch you I will thrash you. You thorn in the foot. You scorpion on the firewood!'

Swinging a large stick over her head, Stepmother raced out from behind one of the charred huts. With a cry, Magoyela sprang away. But she was not quick enough. Stepmother lashed her twice on the back before she could get away. She grew even angrier when she saw me. 'And where have *you* been?'

'We were hiding, My Mother.'

'The rest of us have been back for hours. That is just typical of you, Mulumbe. You dance off into the forest and leave the work to the rest of us.' For some reason, out of all of her husband's children, Stepmother hated me the most.

'They came after us –' I tried to explain.

'Saving your own skin as usual. We could have been taken away for all you cared.'

No, it was not like that, I tried to say. But it was no use defending myself. I never could do any right in her eyes.

'And you have ripped your T-shirt.'

'It was not my fault. The thorns –'

'Well, don't think you will get another. Since you are back at last, you might as well make yourself useful.' Her face creased sourly as though she was chewing a bitter *mululwe* leaf. 'Go and collect some wood for the cooking pot. And then bring me water from the borehole well.'

Collecting wood I found out that the village had been lucky. The marauders had missed some of the grain barns, including one of ours. There would still be some food, although things would get scarce before the next harvest. But that was a long time away. My only worry now was for Tom.

*

Midday and the hot red, sandy earth of the path hurt my feet. The borehole well was half an hour's walk from the village. Usually it was a place for girls and women to linger, to talk and catch up with the news, but today no one had the time for anything other than the briefest exchange of details. I asked everybody I saw if the boys had come back from the hills. No one knew.

'Child Mulumbe, you know what boys are like,' one woman said to me. 'They are like the clouds, they blow anywhere.'

I quickly pumped the water into an old petrol can and lifted it on to my head. Balancing it there with one hand, I set off for home. The sweat stung my eyes like the thorns of the acacia tree. But I did not stop to wipe it away. I had to get back. Perhaps Tom had already returned. I could not rest until I saw him.

I had almost reached the village when I heard the wailing. Distraught voices rose and fell. People were weeping. That could only mean bad news. My heart beat like a bird trapped in a net. Had something happened to Tom? Putting down the water I ran as fast as I could.

'What's going on?' I asked, meeting Magoyela.

'The night marauders have snatched Mutinta.'

'Snatched Mutinta? Are you sure?'

'Yes. Her family has just come back from hiding in the

forest. Mulumbe, has Tom returned yet? He will be very sad. He and Mutinta played *ntuntu* together.'

I could not believe what I was hearing about my friend, Mutinta. A few moons ago, following our old custom of *ntuntu*, she and Tom had gone into the forest together for a while: preparing for marriage. Tom had built her the finest of huts and Mutinta had proudly cooked him the tastiest meals. They had been so happy then, but now I dared not think what had happened to her and Tom. People did not come back when the night marauders took them.

Once I saw a hyena stalk a goat-kid tethered to a hut. As the kid watched the burly scavenger approach, its terrified bleating had frozen my blood. The sound of Mutinta's family's grief reminded me of that bleating. The family held each other so tightly that they seemed a single, sorrowful being. It was only on coming closer that I could pick out the different heads and hands in the tight coil of their sorrow. Mutinta's mother's eyes rolled – red as though stung by a swarm of bees. Her sisters flung their heads back shrieking: 'Where has she gone? Where have they taken our girl? She was as welcome as the rain but now she is lost! We loved her more than dancing but now she is still! She was as pretty as the flowers of the *munimbwa* tree, but now she has been torn from the ground!'

'You fly in the milk, where is the water?' Stepmother had come up behind me.

'My mother, they have taken Mutinta.'

Stepmother's forehead creased cruelly. 'They should have taken you as well. Now bring me that water. After that, pound some maize with that one there.' She pointed to Magoyela. 'And don't think my stick has forgotten that it owes you a beating.'

As we walked to the *ntombo* granary – a little hut placed on stilts to protect it from rats and other scavengers – my younger sister's face look suddenly old. My heart swelled for her.

'Mulumbe,' she said. 'Some of the other boys are back already. But none of them has seen Tom. Do you think he has been hurt as well?'

I took a deep breath. I did not want Magoyela to feel my worry. 'Magoyela, Grandmother says he will be all right.'

'What do *you* say?'

'I say, have you ever known Grandmother to be wrong? Now come on, we must pound the maize into flour.'

Placing some of the cobs in the big bowl of the mortar, we began to grind them with the large pestle: a stick almost the size of Magoyela. It took both of us to lift it up and down. It was hard work.

'Mulumbe,' my sister said after a while. 'Those men

who come in the night – why do they hate us?'

'What else is Crocodile to do with his sharp teeth? Or Rhino, his horn?'

'You sound like Grandmother.'

I looked at my younger sister. She did not understand. Not everyone could talk in pictures. 'They are just cruel people.'

Up and down the pestle beat, slowly crushing the seeds of the cobs into the white flour of mealie meal. It was hot even in the shade beneath the tree where we worked. 'This will make good *nsima*,' I said from time to time, to encourage Magoyela. Usually we would sing, but the grief of Mutinta's family and Tom's absence silenced us.

All at once our rhythm faltered and the pestle struck the side of the mortar. 'Watch out, Magoyela, you are dropping the pestle.' Wide-eyed she was staring at something over my shoulder. 'Is it a snake?' She shook her head. I turned round. A man stood there.

His eyes were bloodshot. His teeth rotten. He looked me steadily in the eye as though I was a goat he was interested in buying. Grunting with self-satisfaction he spat. The globule of sputum flew through the air and landed in the dust close to my feet. I shuddered as though a rat had crossed my path. Even from this distance I could

smell the beer not only coming from his breath but from the very pores of his skin.

It was Olinji, a man known for beating his wives. I began to pound the pestle again, forcing Magoyela to follow my urgent rhythm. When I looked around once more, Olinji had gone. A great relief that I did not fully understand surged through me. It was like when a snake that has been staring at you slides away at last.

But the relief was short-lived. I looked over to where my father sat on his stool outside his hut. Olinji was paying him a visit.

Ever since the time he had lost his eye trying to save my mother, my father had not been the same man. Having married his third wife we no longer seemed to be alive to him. Not caring how we lived or how his youngest wife bullied the rest of us, he lost all interest in farming. Sitting day after day on his stool staring into a distance that only he could see, he would get drunk on buckets of home-brewed beer. Before my mother had been taken he would not even have spoken to Olinji – now the two of them often sat drinking together. During times of want when the rest of the men went to the coal mines to find work, he and Olinji would disappear to the city where they drank and danced with women.

I pounded the mealie meal quicker and quicker.

'Mulumbe,' Magoyela complained, 'do you have to pound so quickly?'

'The quicker we pound, the quicker we'll be finished.'

But I was pounding to stop myself from thinking about my father. To grind to flour the hurt I felt.

'Mulumbe, I cannot keep up with you.'

Seeing how thin Magoyela's arms were, I relented. Ever since her own mother had died, I had tried to look after her. Glancing over at my father, I saw that Step-mother had joined him and Olinji. All three of them seemed to be looking at me.

At first I did not know what was happening. The wailing and crying of Mutinta's family ceased abruptly. After a short, sharp silence, strangled shouts and shrieks erupted. It was only when I heard the joyful bubbling of women ululating that I knew what had happened. Magoyela and I dropped the pestle at the same time. Two figures were coming into the village. I recognised them instantly: Tom and Mutinta. Everyone was running to greet them. Like a forest buck I too sprang towards them.

Tom swept me in his arms. 'My sister,' he whispered. 'I love you.'

He whispered because boys did not like to be heard being affectionate. But I knew he meant what he said.

19

'My brother, we were not worried,' I whispered back. He knew I was lying. I looked at his smile. He was the most handsome boy in the village.

'Your T-shirt is ripped,' he said.

'I escaped with my life,' I replied.

But despite the joy of Mutinta's family and Tom's smile I could see that he carried a heaviness on his shoulders. When I greeted Mutinta she did not reply. She did not even seem to see me. A third person was walking with them. I had not noticed him at first. It was Peter, Tom's best friend and Mutinta's brother.

'*Wabuka*, Peter,' I greeted him.

'*Iyii*,' he replied. '*Wabuka, biyeni*.'

'I am so pleased that your sister returns safely to us.'

He nodded, but there was anxiety in his eyes.

'They took her,' Tom murmured to me. 'We followed them and brought her back.'

I glanced at Mutinta. Her eyes seemed like those of the goat-kid stalked by the hyena. She stumbled and Tom and Peter practically had to carry her to her mother.

Stepmother was waiting for Magoyela and me at the pestle and mortar. 'Why aren't you finished?' she demanded.

'Mutinta is back,' I replied. 'Tom helped rescue her –'

'I don't know why he bothered. I hear he has lost one

of the goats. Who is going to pay for that? You children are just an expense.'

That night, with our hut burnt, I slept outside on the cold ground, sharing Grandmother's blanket. The laughter and ululating of Mutinta's family through the night drowned out the sedate songs of the frogs. But the silvery moon-woman seemed to peer sadly down at us. Even the glittering stars seemed cold and distant. I dreamt that Tom had still not returned and that Grandmother and I were searching the night sky for him, but we found only Olinji. In the dream Olinji's face grew larger and larger until it filled the sky like an angry, burning fire.

GIRL FOR SALE

Although there was much work to do, my father went on one of his drinking trips to the city. Tom built new huts while we girls and women gathered and combed the grass for the roof thatching. Time and time again Stepmother moaned about the loss of the goat. Magoyela got her beating. Stepmother would have beaten Tom too if she dared. Mutinta stayed in her hut with her mother. When Tom had finished the huts and repaired the granaries, he took the goats to the hills. In a week's time he would be starting school again after his holiday.

'Always taking so long to do everything,' Stepmother said one morning after I had drawn water and collected firewood. 'You are useless, just a path that leads nowhere.' Her glare held such hatred that it froze me. But her sudden smile was even colder. 'Today you will go to the fields.'

My heart sank within me. The fields were half a day's walk away from the village. We grew our crops there because it was near the lake. The rains alone rarely gave us enough water. Whoever went to the fields had to stay there for weeks of back-breaking toil: picking stones, weeding and scaring off the birds and wild animals that came to eat the crops. I had been there only recently. It was not my turn. It was Stepmother's turn.

'What is the matter, you dung beetle?' Stepmother demanded. 'Scared of a little work?'

There was no use complaining. 'I shall go and tell Magoyela.'

'Magoyela is not going with you.'

'But Buumi and Simonje are only old enough to scare birds.'

'They are not going either.'

'Just Grandmother and me?'

'You are going by yourself, Mulumbe.'

'By myself?'

'And go now, I don't want you taking all day about it.'

'My Mother, I am going by myself?'

'Am I talking to the frog that repeats the same thing over and over? I need everyone else here. Yes, you are going to the fields by yourself, you stupid girl.'

'But no one ever goes there alone.'

'Go now, before my stick loses its temper.'

'Can I not say goodbye to –'

The stick swung through the air and struck me on the side of my head.

Magoyela and the little ones gathered to wave me goodbye. I could not bring myself to look back at them, but when I felt a tug at my hand I turned to see that little Namaanza had toddled after me. He handed me a gourd. Crouching down I threw my arms around him. Over his shoulder I could see my father's empty stool.

The hoe weighed heavily as I disappeared into the forest. I took with me a goatskin bottle of water, some mealie meal, and an empty petrol canister to use as a cooking pot. The gourd Namaanza had given me was filled with dried seeds. Grandmother had made it. The words she spoke when she first gave it to us echoed in my mind now as I walked alone. *If you find yourself alone in the forest, my little ones, then shake the maraca. Hyena is always looking for a free meal, but ever since Hare played a trick on him by moaning in a high-pitched voice, he does not trust strange noises. If Hyena hears you shaking your maraca he will think it is Hare up to another trick and he will not harm you.*

Even to remember Grandmother's picture-words gave me courage. Shaking the gourd loudly, I looked about. Dangerous places can also be beautiful, especially in the cool of the morning with the rays of the sun-man gentle as laughter. Later he would rage, but now he was

like a father playing with his children. Like my father had once done.

It was growing hot when I heard someone calling my name. 'Mulumbe, Mulumbe!' Waiting uneasily, I shook the rattle. The voice grew louder. 'Mulumbe!'

'Grandmother, *mwabuka*!'

'*Iyii*, Mulumbe.'

'My Grandmother, what are you doing?'

'I am coming with you.'

'But Stepmother said I was to go alone –'

Grandmother swept her away with a gesture. 'Who ever heard of anybody going to the fields alone? It is too dangerous. And lonely. Besides, who else can I play riddles with?' Her old face lit up with a young woman's smile, as though the love between us could cast aside the long years like leaves falling from a tree. 'Girl, I have got such a good one that you will never get it! I dance while sitting down. Who am I?'

'You dance while sitting down?'

'Yes, I dance while sitting down. Who am I?'

I gazed at the forest all around me, thinking. Then I laughed. 'I have found your riddle, Grandmother.'

'Already?'

'You are Tree. When the wind blows Tree dances but he does not move.'

Grandmother laughed too. 'That was too easy, I will find another.' She peered at the canopies of the trees above as though searching.

This was why I loved to play riddles. They transform the whole world. In a game of riddles a well was no longer just a place to draw water, a hoe could not be trusted to simply remain a weeding implement, and even a dung beetle could change into something extraordinary.

'Ah, I have found one!' Grandmother announced.

'Is it a good one?' I replied.

'You will not find this one so easy. When father comes home he will buy us all new clothes. Who is father?'

'When father comes home he will buy us all new clothes?'

As I repeated the words to myself my thoughts flew through the forest like Hornbill investigating everything, searching for the answer. 'Ah!' I exclaimed at last. 'I have found your riddle. Father is springtime.'

'Springtime?'

'In spring the leaves grow on all the trees. They are like new clothes.'

Grandmother looked at me closely then nodded. 'Mulumbe, you are a very clever girl. But why are you grinning?'

'Because I have found a riddle for *you*.'

'Ah! Is it a good one?'

'Maybe even you won't be able to guess it, Grandmother.' I smiled. I had never been able to make up a riddle that she could not work out. Nobody had. 'Grandmother, here is my riddle. I am the little boy who conquered the chief at the conference. Who am I?'

'You are the little boy who conquered the chief at the conference?'

Grandmother made a big show of thinking. She narrowed her eyes and rubbed her chin until I burst into laughter. She always did this, even if she knew the answer straightaway. Whispering to herself, Grandmother began to solve the puzzle. 'The little boy must be something small that can overcome something big.' She narrowed her eyes some more and rubbed her chin. 'Ah, I have found the answer. The little boy is the dry streambed that lies near our village.'

'The dry streambed?'

'Yes, and the chief is the big log that lies on that dry bed. You know the one?'

'Yes, Grandmother. I know it.'

'Nothing can move that log. Not even ten men working together. It is too heavy. A chief amongst logs. A king amongst tree trunks. And the dry bed, those grains of sand, how could they lift Chief Log? They can't even stand up against a little gust of wind or a child's foot. But

in the rainy season that dry bed will become a raging torrent dragging the old log so far away that we will never see it again. The streambed is the little boy.'

'Grandmother,' I laughed. 'You have *not* found the answer.'

Pretending to be annoyed, Grandmother shook her head. 'I can see I'm going to have to give this one a lot of thought.'

As we walked it grew hotter. The sun-man raged with anger and even the trees of the forest could do little to shield us from his pounding fists. Every step became an effort, as though we were wading through the shallows of the lake that lay close to the fields. Everything throbbed with heat. A pulsating silence stifled the forest except for the insects rasping like seeds in the gourd. Only the riddles helped us forget the sweat scalding our eyes, the hard work waiting for us at the fields, and also, for a fleeting instant, the fear that still clung to us all after the visit from the night marauders.

'Ah, I have found the answer!' announced Grandmother at last. 'The little boy is an elephant. When an elephant is born he is only small. Fully grown who can stand against him?'

'No, no!' I clapped my hands in delight. 'You have *NOT* found the answer.'

Grandmother had still not guessed it by the time we arrived.

The marauders had not been here. Our crops were untouched. The field hut still stood. Tom had built it last year so that those staying at the fields could have a roof over their heads. It would be our home for the next few weeks. I looked over the familiar landscape of tall mealie corn and millet. All the families of our village raised their crops here and the view was sparsely dotted with figures patiently bending and lifting as they worked. From time to time a child's voice was raised to scare a scavenging bird.

That night Grandmother cooked our *nsima*. When we had eaten we sat round the fire on which we placed sprigs of the *mutandamasenya* tree to make the sweet smoke that keeps the mosquitoes away. In the flames I saw the faces of those I had been forced to leave behind. Tom smiling at the thought of a new term at school as he herded the goats in the hills, Magoyela worried by Stepmother's stick, Buumi, Luuwo, and Simonje laughing, and Namaanza, who was little more than a baby, reaching out to pull my nose . . .

'Poor Hare,' Grandmother suddenly said. I looked up from the faces in the fire to hers. It was wreathed in shadows from the flickering flames. But nothing sparkled brighter than her eyes. 'Mulumbe, why is it that all the other animals want to catch him?'

'I do not know, Grandmother.' I smiled. This was one of her ways of beginning a story. She must have sensed my homesickness.

'So much smaller than the others, what is little Hare to do?'

'He could use some tricks.'

'Tricks, Mulumbe?'

I nodded and she smiled.

'Yes, girl, I suppose he might be able to think up some tricks.'

For a long time she stared into the fire as though searching for a story there. The silence that always preceded one of Grandmother's tales lay as deeply as the waters of the lake near to which our fields lay. Even the moon-woman seemed to bend down closer as though waiting for the story to begin. In the vast stillness of the stars and Grandmother, it was as though the whole of creation was straining itself to hear. Only the flames moved, dancing to their own rhythm. 'Mulumbe,' she began at last, 'something very funny happened once.'

'What happened, Grandmother?'

'It was a long, long time ago. In fact I am not telling you a lie when I say that it all happened when I was a girl

of about your age. It was the dry season and one by one all the water holes dried up. Lion decided that something had to be done. *Listen to me everyone,* declared the King of the Beasts when he had summoned all the animals, *we are going to have to dig a well.'*

Grandmother used a different voice for each animal as though calling her characters, one by one, out of the shadows where the vast night-time met the small circle of fire.

'All the animals agreed to dig the well together,' Grandmother continued. 'Except for one. *Count me out,* Hare said, boldly twitching his long ears right in front of Lion's nose. *That sounds too much like hard work.* The others were outraged.

'If you don't do any of the work then you won't be allowed to drink when the well is finished, the King of the Beasts bellowed. With a shrug Hare ambled off into the hills.

'At last, after many days' hard labour the animals had finished their well. The water was the sweetest they had ever tasted. *We will have to set a guard at night,* decided Lion, *just in case that no-good Hare tries to quench his thirst here.* Since Elephant was the strongest he took the first watch. Sure enough Hare appeared just as the moon rose in the sky. Whistling his favourite tune he strolled over to the waterhole. Elephant's blood boiled at the sight. *Go*

 31

away, you lazy good-for-nothing, he trumpeted. Hare was holding a gourd. He dipped his fingers into it and licked them lovingly. *Oh yes,* he chuckled dreamily, *what a sweet taste!* The elephant stared at him. *What have you got in that gourd?* he demanded. *Nothing,* replied Hare, *just a little honey.* Now, as you know, no animal can resist honey. *Let me have a taste,* Elephant begged. Hare shook his head. *I am afraid only those whose hands are tied can taste,* he said. *Then tie mine up,* demanded Elephant. With the guard safely tied up, Hare drank from the well to his heart's content. *What about my honey?* Elephant asked, but he realised that he had been tricked. The next morning when Elephant told the others how his strength had been out-manoeuvred they grew enraged. *I'll stand watch tonight,* said Hippo. But Hare tricked him in exactly the same way. He went on to trick each animal in turn: Lion, Zebra, Giraffe, Hyena. *I'll stand guard tonight,* Tortoise said at last. The other animals snorted dismissively. *What can you do, small one?* demanded Lion. *If Hare has tricked us more important animals, how on earth will you stop him?* Tortoise replied: *I have a plan. And here it is . . .'*

There was a rustle in the shadows beyond the circle of light. I turned, half-expecting tortoise's wizened face to be peering at us, but there was nothing, just the calling of the night frogs and stars glimmering in the sky.

'That night,' Grandmother chuckled, continuing with the tale, 'Hare found no guard at the well so he set himself to drink his fill. But just as he did so a small voice called out, *Hey you, big ears, leave my water alone!* When Hare saw Tortoise, he burst into laughter. But Tortoise challenged him again. *Long lugs, I said get your dirty snout out of my water!* Hare stepped over. *Don't annoy me, you dung beetle,* he warned Tortoise, *or I will fight you.* But before he could return to the water Tortoise declared, *I think your ears look stupid.* When Hare tried to push Tortoise away he found that his paw had stuck to his shell. He made to kick himself free but found that his back paw was also stuck. Tortoise had covered himself with tree glue. The more Hare struggled, the more he became stuck. *I've caught him!* shouted Tortoise. All the other animals rushed out from their hiding places and Hare saw he was trapped. He could not even twitch his beautiful long ears. Unable to escape he began to whimper and whine. *You can do what you like with me. You can tear me limb from limb, swallow me whole or bite me into bits. But please don't pull me from Tortoise's shell and throw me on to that soft sand. I would hate that more than anything.* Of course that was exactly what all the animals wanted to do: the thing that Hare would hate more than anything else. So Elephant tugged him free from Tortoise's shell and

with one kick Zebra sent him through the air. Hare landed on the soft sand, rolled a somersault, and ran free. *Thank you, my friends*, he called in parting. *You are very helpful! I'll see you tonight when I get thirsty.* And off he went, humming his favourite tune.'

I clapped my hands in delight. 'Ah! How clever Hare is. Please tell me another story about him.'

'I think you must have heard all his stories by now, child.'

'Just one more, Grandmother.'

'We have a hard day tomorrow. Now we must sleep. Even Hare must sleep so that he can dream up new tricks.'

The next day I was so hard at work hoeing among the mealie corn that I did not hear the steps of the person approaching from behind. Suddenly their shadow darkened the earth at my feet. 'And how are you today, young woman?' It was Stepmother. I looked around for Grandmother. But she had gone to the lake for water.

'M-my M-mother, I am well,' I stammered. Not only did her presence confuse me, but also her greeting. Usually she insulted me.

'It is good to see you, my beautiful young woman.' The tone of Stepmother's voice seemed friendly. Her

mouth had managed to twist itself into a smile. But when she stepped aside to show who was with her my heart beat like a bird caught by the wings. 'Now my young woman with beautiful eyes, say hello to Olinji.'

It was as though a ghost had stepped out from the tall mealie corn. A ghost with rotten teeth, and a self-satisfied smile. A ghost stinking of beer. I stepped back in horror and curtseyed.

'See how hard this young woman works,' Stepmother boasted to Olinji. Grabbing my hands she held them out. 'Look, they are bleeding.'

Olinji nodded and spat. The globule of his spit plumped the dust near my foot like a dung beetle.

'Now, my beautiful young woman,' Stepmother said. 'Come with us to the hut. Olinji has something to say to you.'

Stepmother was still smiling but her fingernails dug deep into my hand. Not only had she made the journey here but she had brought two stools. What was going on? The two stools had been placed side by side outside the field hut. Olinji sat down on one. He slapped a fly that had landed on his neck. A sickening stench of sour beer wafted over me.

'Mulumbe,' began Stepmother. 'You are no longer a girl. In fact, you are ready to marry.' Olinji let out a

mewling grunt of approval. 'Mulumbe, I have found a husband who will offer us a good price for you, a good *luselo.*' Her words dug even deeper into me than her fingernails. 'Mulumbe, Olinji has sent a message to your father. He has agreed to pay two goats and three hens. And some money too. It is a very good bride price. Olinji knows that you are a hard worker. He knows that he will be getting a bargain. And you will accept. That is why I have brought the stools.'

The ground beneath my feet seemed to spin. I looked down at the stool but all I saw was a swarm of dancing dots, as though I was gazing directly into the sun. My father had made this stool for me before the night marauders had come and taken his wife and his eye. I had watched him make it, first gathering the wood then fashioning it painstakingly. He had poured his love into it, but now it was going to be where I met my doom. I knew the custom well. The moment I sat down on this stool, was the moment I agreed to marry this man.

Stepmother was grinning like Baboon when he finds juicy grubs under a rock. 'Mulumbe, sit down with Olinji.'

I looked around wildly for help.

'Mulumbe,' Stepmother's tone sharpened. 'Sit with your husband.'

Olinji held out a hand. The forefinger flicked at me

like the tongue of a snake. 'Come here.'

'Yes.' Although it was me speaking I did not seem to recognise my own voice.

'Sit down, little wife.'

'Yes.' I heard the word again, but this time it was *definitely* not me speaking.

All at once Stepmother staggered. Something had pushed her out of the way. When I looked down at the stool someone else was sitting in my place. 'Grandmother!' I gasped.

'My husband is too kind to offer me this seat to sit on,' Grandmother said.

'Husband?' Olinji's mouth fell wide open.

'Yes, you have just asked me to sit on your wedding stool.'

'Me?'

'Are there any other men here?' Although her face was as wrinkled as Tortoise's, Grandmother's eyes twinkled.

'Old mother you are sitting in someone else's seat!' Stepmother hissed.

'But I don't understand,' said Grandmother. 'This man said: *Sit down, little wife*. What else am I supposed to do but sit?'

'He didn't mean you.'

'But *you* are already married, wife of my son.'

'He doesn't want to marry me either!'

'So it must be me. This child here is far too young for a big important man like Olinji.'

Having spoken, Grandmother began to hum her favourite tune just like Hare often did in her stories. Olinji's eyes bulged until I thought they would pop. Stepmother bubbled with rage. 'Old woman you are deliberately trying to sabotage my plans. Olinji has agreed *luselo*. Get up from the stool so that –'

'Already agreed *luselo*! He is keen.' Grandmother giggled like a girl. 'Tell Olinji that I am too old to bear him any sons. But if he is happy to ignore my age then I am too.' She turned to me: 'Mulumbe, Olinji has agreed a *luselo* for me.'

'Not for you,' Olinji spluttered.

'He must really want me. Just wait until I get back to the village and tell everyone about Olinji offering *luselo* for an old woman like me. I wonder what they will say? Perhaps everyone will laugh at him.'

Panic flared Olinji's nostrils as he stood up.

With the grace of a girl Grandmother also stood. 'Perhaps I have made a mistake and these are not marriage stools. Perhaps Olinji will take these stools back to the village. Perhaps I will not be able to tell everyone that he wanted to marry me, the oldest woman in the village.'

Kicking aside his stool Olinji ran into the forest. With a shriek of rage Stepmother seized the stools and ran after him. Grandmother and I burst into laughter. 'Grandmother,' I said, 'you are just like Hare.'

Her eyes twinkled. 'Even when Hare is old he still thinks up new tricks.'

I AM SILENT, BUT I BRING THE STORM

We had been at the fields for about a week when Grandmother let me sleep until just before dawn. 'I must go and collect wood,' I said rising quickly.

'I have already collected it, Mulumbe.'

'Then let me fetch the water.'

'That has been brought too.'

'But, Grandmother, why have you let me sleep while you did all the work?'

She took my hand gently and led me outside. The fire was lit and the *nsima* was already cooking. 'Mulumbe,' she whispered, 'today is a special day.'

Sitting down, I waited for her to explain. But she did not. Instead she said: 'Mulumbe, I have a riddle for you.'

'This is early for a game of riddles,' I laughed.

'This is no game, Mulumbe.'

She ladled out our *nsima*. I blew to cool it. 'I am silent,' said Grandmother. 'But I bring the storm.'

'You are silent but you bring the storm?'

She nodded. 'Who am I?'

I looked up at the sky. Soon the sun would rise. Already I could see that there might be hope of rain. 'That is easy, Grandmother. I am a cloud. Clouds are silent but they bring the storm that washes everything away.'

'But clouds rattle with thunder, Mulumbe. Try again.'

As I was thinking, the first golden trickle of sunlight woke the hornbills. They began to chatter and the riddle seemed even more impossible to understand. Everything was too peaceful to think about a storm. I made a few more guesses, but could not really think too hard about it. Also, the look in Grandmother's eyes confused me. It was not sadness. Nor was it joy. But something in-between those two. What had she meant when she said that today was special?

Grandmother was pointing at the ground. 'What do you see, girl?'

I looked hard but could not see anything. She continued to point, standing motionless above me. Slowly, as the light of morning grew, a shape formed in the red earth. 'An elephant print!'

'He passed last night, my child, when we were sleeping.'

'Ah, Grandmother, we were lucky.'

She nodded. 'That is why I know that this is a special

day. Look how close he came to the hut. One step in that direction and we might never have woken.'

'Now I see the answer to the riddle, Grandmother. Although he is the biggest animal to tread the earth, Elephant walks silently upon it. I am silent, but I bring the storm. I am Eleph–' Without even finishing my sentence I rushed over to where the crops grew. A single elephant on the rampage can destroy the fields of a whole village in one morning.

Grandmother found me gazing at the field in relief. All our crops were still standing. 'Yes, Mulumbe,' the old woman whispered. 'Last night Elephant passed on without stopping. The storm passed overhead. When I saw this I realised how lucky the day was. That is why today I have decided to –' She broke off and looked at me in a way I had never seen before. 'All in good time, child, I will tell you all in good time.'

The crops were growing. The cobs plumping. If the rains were good this year then there would be enough to eat in the village even though most of our granaries had been emptied by the night marauders. Our spirits rose as we walked to the lake to collect water together. We sang about how beautiful the morning was, how lucky we had been to avoid Elephant, and how we looked forward to tasting the first mealie cobs. In the middle of a verse,

Grandmother suddenly fell silent and on to her face came that same, baffling expression I had noticed earlier. 'Yes, this is a good day for it,' I heard her whisper to herself.

As always, we smelt the lake before we saw it. The scent of water in a dry land eases the heart like the shade of a *musikili* tree at noon. Before we saw the lake, we also heard it: a long ringing cry, the call of Fishing Eagle. Strong yet delicate as a feather, this was the song of the lake.

We mounted a rise of land and there was the water spread out before us, shimmering under the early morning sun like the wings of a giant blue butterfly. I followed Grandmother down to the shore, checking that Crocodile was not hiding close by disguised as a log. Fishing Eagle was busy at work. She hovered high above the water then plunged, talons first. For a few moments she seemed to be struggling to untie a knot of water only to emerge with a haul of pure silver that twisted and turned in her talons as the bird flew away. Fishing Eagle had caught her prey. 'Mulumbe,' Grandmother whispered, 'what do you see?'

'I see the lake, Grandmother,' I replied, puzzled by the question.

'What else?'

'I see Fishing Eagle.'

'What else?'

'Is this another riddle, Grandmother?'

The water near the shores was dotted with dead trees whose bare branches stretched up out of the water. My eyes flew over the familiar sight like Fishing Eagle searching for something new, but there was nothing for them to perch on except for the trees. 'I see the trees, Grandmother,' I said uncertainly.

The odd look glinted in her eyes again: strange, faraway. 'What are those trees?'

In one of the trees was a nest of jumbled sticks. Fishing Eagle landed on it with her catch. And all at once her cry seemed to fill the whole world. 'They are like people,' I heard myself mumbling. 'The trees stand like people in the water with their arms outstretched.'

In a movement so quick and graceful that it might have belonged to Fishing Eagle, Queen of the Skies, Grandmother bent down and with both hands scooped water from the lake. She cast it high and I watched in wonder as the drops, turned silver by the sun, twisted through themselves then fell, breaking over me in a lovely, cooling, baptising dowse. 'Mulumbe,' she whispered, 'today *is* the day.'

When we returned to the fields, the red earth, already parched by the sun, gratefully drank what we gave. The rains would have to come soon if we were going to have a good crop. We had been hoeing for a while when I heard something rustling deep within the mealie maize. One of the stalks danced as though something was being plucked from it. A chewing sound followed.

Picking up a round stone I fitted it to the sling we always kept at hand when in the fields. We had to be careful. Once a warthog broke Magoyela's arm. She had screamed for a whole day. Another stalk quivered. The chewing sound followed. Then a cheeky face peered out. 'Baboon!' I shouted.

'Quick, stop the thief!' Grandmother yelled, dropping her hoe and running over.

The thief shoved another plump mealie cob in his mouth. The sling circled my head three times then I let fly. The stone landed close to the insolent face. With a cry Baboon crashed away through the mealie stalks. The second stone whirred into the crops. 'And don't come back again,' Grandmother shouted. 'You stupid thieving monkey!' Which was the worst insult anyone can give to Baboon who considers himself superior to mere monkeys.

As we were examining the limited damage, I noticed a woven gourd of dried grass hanging by a single thread from a tall mealie stalk. 'Ah Grandmother,' I whispered in awe. 'A weaver bird's nest!' We looked at it in silence, as intricate and beautiful as any of the baskets that our women made. 'But how do the parents come in and out?' I asked.

'Watch.'

There was a flash of yellow, brilliant as the sun. Cool air fanned across my face.

'Mulumbe, mother bird has come back.'

A tiny bird had flown to the base of the beautiful grass gourd and squeezed inside through a small hole. Her arrival was greeted by a chirruping within. The young ones were being fed.

'There,' said Grandmother. 'Even Weaverbird knows that today is the day.'

It was when we looked up from the nest that we saw Elephant.

The huge beast was no more than a slingshot away but he had not noticed us. He pulled up whole plants and lifted them into his mouth. Even if Elephant had decided to charge, neither of us could have moved. We were both stuck fast, like Hare on Tortoise's shell.

Grandmother came round first. 'Mulumbe,' she whispered, 'move back very slowly.'

But still I could not break out of the spell cast over me by the sheer size of the animal. Legs thick as a tree trunk, feet wide enough to crush us like beetles, his tusks almost reached to the ground. Yet his eyes were tiny, as though they belonged only to a bird of the air, not the strongest beast to walk the earth. And all the time he was eating his way towards us until we could see the red dust on his back where he had been rolling. When was he going to notice us?

Grandmother's gentle caress brought me out of the trance. 'Mulumbe,' she breathed into my ear, 'come with me and don't make any sudden movements.'

We began to edge away. Elephant continued to eat. 'That's it,' Grandmother coaxed. 'Keep moving, child.'

Reaching a tree we hid behind it. Already Elephant had eaten more than a whole troop of baboons could in the same time. Tears scalded my eyes. 'It's not fair.'

Grandmother stroked my head. 'Troubled times are coming.'

Troubled times. I knew what such words meant. Three years before, the rains had failed and the crops had not grown. My little brother, Kapu had grown weaker and weaker through lack of food, until he no longer even had the strength to knock away the flies that landed on his lips. Two rainy seasons had been all he would ever know of this great world with its forests and hornbills. Who would die this time? The old and the very young go first.

I dashed out from behind the tree. 'Mulumbe,' Grandmother cried. 'Where are you going?'

'I am going to stop him.'

'But no one can stop Elephant.'

'I must try!'

Each mealie stalk he ripped up brought hunger nearer. I fitted a stone to my sling. The sling sang as it circled my head. Once, twice, thrice. 'Missed!' I hissed under my breath. Elephant had still not even noticed me. My second shot struck him on the back.

The great beast looked about for the hidden attacker.

'Mulumbe!' shouted Grandmother breaking cover. 'What are you doing, girl?' For the first time in my life I saw Grandmother overcome with fear.

My hand shook as I fitted another missile. It was as large a stone as I could manage and it struck the immense animal on the head. At last he saw us. When tranquil, Elephant moves without a sound as though passing through a restful dream, but now, flapping his ears, he trumpeted thunderously. The ground shook beneath my feet as he gouged it with his huge tusks then began to charge. The storm was breaking.

'Run, Grandmother,' I shouted, waving my arms so that the enraged animal followed me. 'Run!'

He was so close now that I could smell his sharp

musk. It smothered me like the smoke from the sprigs of the *mutandamasenya* tree enveloping the mosquitoes. The red dust he kicked up filled my mouth to choking. There was no hope. Any moment now he was going to crush me.

It was then that I heard Grandmother's voice talking inside my head. 'Mulumbe,' she urged, 'do you remember the way Hare ran when Elephant was chasing him? He did not run in a straight line.'

'I remember, he zigzagged.'

Darting to the left, I felt the swirl of air as Elephant rumbled past, his huge bulk vibrating the earth where I would have been. I kept running but within moments he had managed to turn and was bearing down on me again. Nearer and nearer he came until the animal's hot breath was suffocating. Surely this time I could not evade him. I flung myself to the right. And closed my eyes. There was a crash. The beast had charged into a tree, it split with a shattering clap.

I escaped with my life, but I could not prevent Elephant from destroying our crops. Having chased me away he returned to our field and ate his fill. The strongest of all beasts is not to be stopped by a sling.

We were not the only unlucky ones. A little later the

rest of the herd arrived. By midday every field had been stripped of their crops. The sounds of mourning and grief drifted thickly on the air like smoke, as they had done when Mutinta was feared lost. But this time there would be no healing ululations of joy. The visit of the elephants meant hunger and death. As I gazed at the destroyed crops I saw the little face of my lost brother, Kapu. He had slipped slowly from life until only his eyes showed the life within. Then, one morning, they too had closed, like a door that we can never open again. Was the same thing now going to happen to Namaanza or Luuwo, or even Magoyela?

THE PEOPLE OF THE GREAT RIVER

'Mulumbe,' said Grandmother breaking into my sorrowful thoughts, 'we must start work.'

'Work?' I gestured at the flattened crops. 'Everything has been destroyed.' In my despair I felt like lying down motionless with the fallen mealie stalks.

Her voice was calm but her eyes were gleaming. 'Child, first we are going to clear away the debris. Then we are going to plough the earth again.'

'Plough?'

'Yes. Clear and plough as we always do when we till the earth. But before we begin, you must tell me that riddle again.' She took my hand. 'The one you gave me as we walked to the fields. The one I have not found yet.'

'Grandmother, how can this be a time for riddles?'

'Tell me it again,' she insisted. There was great hunger in her voice.

The words seemed meaningless as I repeated the riddle. 'I am the little boy who conquered the chief at

the conference. Who am I?'

She stared at me for a long time then nodded. 'Mulumbe, for the first time I cannot find the answer.'

I had saved up this riddle lovingly, cherishing it, looking forward to testing Grandmother. But I felt no triumph, only a strange, hungry sadness. I spoke without tone: 'The little boy is sleep, Grandmother. Although the chief is the most important man, even he cannot resist sleep.'

'Sleep? Ah, that is a good riddle. You are a clever girl.' Still holding my hand, she raised it to her face and laid it against her cheek. 'Your riddle tells the truth. The things that seem weak can conquer the powerful. Although we are weak now, somehow we must conquer our misfortune. We must grow a second crop. And we must begin now by clearing the land again.'

Exploding with sudden energy like the *nkulyukulyu* starlings breaking from the bush at dawn, Grandmother bustled over to the shattered crops. 'If we work hard there is still time for another crop to grow.'

My voice cracked. 'But the rains will not last that long.'

'Mulumbe, we have the lake –'

'Grandmother, the amount of water we can carry from the lake will not be enough for the crops unless a long rainy season follows. You know how thirsty the mealie grows.'

She started to pile the fallen mealie stalks and pull up the stubble of the destroyed crop by the root. She worked as hard as two young women and as I watched her my love for her became painful, like a thorn that is lodged in the flesh. When I could bear that pain no longer I went over and began to work alongside her.

The sun grew hotter and hotter until it was like Elephant sitting on us. The others who had lost their crops gathered round us. 'What are you doing?' they asked in disbelief.

Grandmother's reply was to work even harder.

'You are wasting your time,' they said. 'Even if you can grow a second crop, the rains will not last to nourish it.' They looked at us as though we were mad then drifted silently away into the forest. Everybody was going back to the village. Grandmother made us hats from thick leaves so that we could work through the hottest part of the day. The scalding sweat ran into our eyes, blinding us, until we could not see the maize roots we pulled, but still we toiled, working by touch, every grip and tug a torture to my bleeding hands.

Towards evening, when the sun-man had spent the worst of his pitiless fury and was growing old and gentle, I found the weaverbirds' nest. It had been crushed flat. All the skill and artistry of the parents had not been able to

protect the little nestlings. They lay scattered on the ground close by. The life had already dried from them, and my tears, dotting the thirsty ground, could not cause it to flow again. Savagely I clawed my tears away.

'No,' said Grandmother gently. 'Do not stop your tears. They will water the ground and keep your heart soft. There must always be tears as well as laughter. Now it is the time for sorrow. But one day laughter *will* come back. And we must be ready for its return.'

That evening Grandmother and I were the only ones left at the fields. The flames of our cooking fire were a lonely light in the night. Every mouthful of *nsima* we ate made me think of the hunger that the days ahead might hold. Never had I seen Grandmother looking so old.

Even the moon-woman was pale and thin, as though she too could see the coming of a time of hunger.

'Mulumbe,' Grandmother said, breaking our long silence. 'Have you remembered that today is a special day?'

'A special day?'

'Yes.'

I stared in amazement at Grandmother. The flickering shadows of the fire appeared now to be smoothing away her exhaustion and softening the deep lines on her face. She was no longer bowed down but sat bolt upright, so that the immense night hovering above the circle of light seemed to be kept back by the power of her shoulders. As she looked at me that strange, puzzling expression I had noticed earlier in the day returned to her eyes. It was as though Fishing Eagle herself was looking at me, and could see everything. 'Grandmother, how can this be a special day?'

'Girl, what has happened today makes me certain. You escaped Elephant, riding the storm where others would have perished. But also a time of want is coming. And I cannot see beyond it. Mulumbe, I think that my days are short. The moment has come for me to give you your inheritance. That is why it is a special day.'

'No, you will be all right. You will survive. You will –'

'Already the vulture is circling. Before the rains come again, he will find my bones.'

My voice echoed in the vast night. 'You cannot leave me alone!' The tears scorched my eyes, bitter as thorns. 'What will my life be like without you?

'Today is special because the time has come for me to give you the story.'

I stared at her in disbelief. 'Story?'

She nodded. 'That is what I am going to give you. A story. Your inheritance. Something far more important than just one life.'

'How can a story be more important than a person?'

'Mulumbe, this story is not about clever Hare or Hyena. It is the story of the lake, of those trees that stand in it. It is the story of our people. Perhaps you could say this story *is* our people. For sometimes only stories are strong enough to carry the truth.'

'Grandmother, today I understand nothing.'

A sudden movement fanned the flames into a dance as though Fishing Eagle had taken flight from beside us. Grandmother had stood up. Staring at the great night sky above, she stretched her arms so high that I thought she was going to pluck the stars down from heaven and offer them to me in the palm of her hand. Her silhouette was like one of the trees in the lake. 'Mulumbe, have you ever heard the old ones talking of a different life?'

'A different life?'

'We have not always lived here: where the soil is thin and the rain thinner; where every year hunger and disease takes one child from a family.'

'Yes, Grandmother. I *have* heard the old ones talk of this better life.' I recalled the stories about how our people had once lived in a better place.

'And did you believe these stories, Mulumbe?'

I hesitated.

Grandmother's sigh was as soft as butterfly wings.

'The old speak of things from many rainy seasons ago, and time seems to shrivel the truth just like the dry white season shrivels the leaves. But still, the stories are true. And soon there will be no one left who remembers how it really was. The past will be forgotten. The coming time of want will bleach the bones of a great injustice dry. That is why tonight I am giving you your inheritance: the true story of your people.'

Half fear, half excitement stole over me. I could no longer look at Grandmother.

'Mulumbe, once our people *did* live in a good land. Our huts were on the banks of a swift-flowing river. We ate fish whenever we wanted, not like today when we must buy a fishing licence that no one can afford. There our gardens gave us many wonderful vegetables that will not flourish in this fruitless soil. The earth was fertile, every year we grew two crops. Rarely were flies seen to stitch together the mouths of hungry children. If wild animals bothered us, we were allowed to kill them. We built our huts on both sides of this river; staying on this side for a while, then going to the other as took our fancy, crossing the river in canoes cut from the *muunga* tree. And that is how we got our name. Everybody called us 'the People of the Great River'.'

The fire cracked. The night frogs called. Rocking back

 57

and forth Grandmother began to sing softly. 'How lovely is our river. Its touch fills me with joy. I want to sit on its banks forever and watch the *kadondwe* cormorant dive.' Her voice grew too faint for me to hear until all at once her singing became a loud chant: 'What's this I see? Who is this coming to our riverbank? He is a stranger. He is not the *kadondwe* cormorant who sings as she dives. The stranger is speaking. The stranger is telling us that we must move. The stranger is saying that they are going to kill the river. The stranger is saying that no longer can the people and the *kadondwe* cormorant live beside the river, their great mother.' The song grew urgent. Grandmother's voice flared with the flames. 'Now I see the river growing. Growing beyond its banks. The people are fleeing. Fleeing from the rising waters of a river that has died and become . . . The river has become a mouth devouring what we know . . . The river is a lake! Where is the *kadondwe* cormorant? Where are the People of the Great River? Only the trees are left, dead, their arms stretched out, they are calling for the people to come back and sit beneath them once more.'

Grandmother stopped singing and took my hand. 'Mulumbe, when I was a girl of your age, they dammed the river. They moved us all in the back of trucks to new, poorer lands whose soil would not grow the old crops.

The river became the lake. They drowned our village. The trees you see in the water, where Fishing Eagle makes her nest, were once the forest I walked through as a little girl with my Grandfather. And such a forest, full of great riches! At that time my mother and brothers were staying on the other side of the river. I never saw them again. It was a long time ago, but I remember it. And the truck shook us as it drove through the bush, grinding us as though we were mealie flour.'

She buried her face in her hands; but when she looked up, there was no sorrow in her eyes. A strange peace had calmed her. 'Yes, Mulumbe, this is a special day. I have waited many years for this moment. Now I know that the truth will not die.' A smile blossomed on her face, quick and beautiful as the flowers that an hour's rain teases from the dry earth even after the longest drought. Looking beyond the circle of firelight she cupped her ear as though listening.

'Grandmother,' I whispered, 'what can you hear?'

'Listen with me.'

'I can't hear anything.'

'Listen, child. Can't you hear the river flowing again? I am standing here on its banks like I did when I was a child. I can hear its murmur. I can see the *kadondwe* cormorant dive.'

'How, Grandmother?' I asked. 'How can you hear the murmur of the river? How can you –?'

'Come stand with me by the river.'

The old woman began singing again. It seemed to be a song that a child might sing. Then she began to dance nimbly and I realised that once again she was a little girl standing on the banks of the river. Still she sang, and the tune lulled me like the music of flowing water.

I must have fallen asleep, rocked by the vision of my Grandmother as a girl standing by the river, because the next thing I knew, the moon-woman had wandered higher in the sky and the stars were even brighter. Grandmother was still singing, but her song had changed. 'What is happening?' she chanted. 'What is this I see? Someone will not leave the village. Who is it that I see sitting on his stool? Sitting on his stool as the water rises. Who will I never see again? Taken from us by the rising waters? I will never see the wise one again.' The chanting stopped. 'Mulumbe?' Grandmother said.

'Yes, Grandmother.'

'Not everyone left as they were ordered when they built the dam. My Grandfather refused to leave. And just like the *kadondwe* cormorant, we never saw him again. He disappeared beneath the waters, never to surface. And with him, the old ways drowned too. But when

I see the outstretched arms of the drowned trees . . . I remember . . .'

Leaning behind her, Grandmother threw more wood on to the fire. The night that had been creeping closer during the singing and the telling of the story leapt back.

As the flames roared, Grandmother's age-lines tightened again, biting deeper into her skin. I could no longer see the girl standing on the bank of a river – just a tired old woman. 'Yes, today is a special day,' she said, 'because today the story will live on.'

'But why have you given it to me, Grandmother?' I cried.

'Who else should I give it to?'

'Someone important. Someone like Tom. I am just a girl. I do not even go to school.'

'Mulumbe, the river of our ancestors flows most strongly through you. Girl, remember your riddle, real strength is found in those who might be thought to be weak.'

'I do not understand.'

'One day you will, my child. Because you must. And maybe one day you too will hear the river flowing again, telling its tale of our lives. Maybe one day stories of plenty will be told again by the People of the Great River.'

A LAND OF SNAKES . . .

Grandmother and I were not to remain alone at the fields for long. The next day as we worked, a figure came out from the trees. He ran over and threw his arms round me. 'Oh, Tom,' I cried. 'We have lost everything!'

To my surprise Tom began to laugh. 'Everything? No. My sister and her Grandmother are still alive. I did not know what I would find when I arrived. People told me about the rogue elephant. Is it still around?'

'No. The whole herd has moved on.'

'My sister, I am so happy.'

'Happy? But my brother, look!' I pointed at the gouged earth and heap of broken mealie stalks we had piled high. 'The crop is finished.'

He was still smiling. 'Then it is just as well I came. You are really going to need my help now.'

'Does Stepmother know you are here?' I asked.

'My sister, what has it got to do with that one?'

'And what about school?'

'School has been delayed for another week. Now come. Let's see if I can work as hard as you. I have brought more seeds.'

Together the three of us cleared the land. Then, with no ox to do the job, Tom had to haul the plough himself. Often he would stumble and fall face down in the crumbling, red earth. Each time he got up with a wide grin.

A few days later someone else came back to the fields. It was Peter. '*Wabuka, biyeni,* Mulumbe,' he greeted me.

'*Iyii,*' I replied.

He grinned. 'I should have known that even Elephant is no match for Mulumbe Mudenda.'

'Is Mutinta with you?'

He shook his head, and although he tried to hide it, I could see the sadness in his eyes. 'Mutinta stays in her hut. She only talks to her mother.' I watched him as he walked slowly over to his own family's field, the hoe bouncing on his shoulder.

When the ploughing was done, Grandmother and I sowed our new seeds. 'Grow! Grow! Grow!' we sang placing them in the red earth, each one a tiny but powerful wish. 'Grow and have babies, ten cobs on each stalk!'

'Just you wait and see, Mulumbe,' Grandmother said. 'The Weaverbird will build her nest again. It will be like when we lived at the river and had two crops every year.'

When we had finished sowing, clouds gathered overhead. 'Come rain! Come rain! Come rain again!' Grandmother and I sang staring at the sky. But the sky grew blue once more.

The next morning it clouded over again. Feeling a spot of rain, Grandmother and I looked up. Moments later we began to laugh and shout like children. Tom dropped his plough where he was turning over new earth and ran over. 'It's raining!' he shouted. 'It's raining!'

Arms stretched out, heads thrown back, we danced in the heavy rain. Opening our mouths wide we drank the welcome water.

During this time of new planting the rain fell regularly and refreshingly. Day by day more people came back from the village until the fields were full of song and life.

At last it was time for us to return to the village.

My welcome from Stepmother was bitter. 'Why did you bother to come back, you leaking gourd?'

'We have replanted what Elephant destroyed –'

'Since you lost everything else, you might have had the decency to lose yourself.'

At least Magoyela and my other little sisters and brothers were overjoyed to see us. I had to kiss and lift each one in turn, then show them how me, Grandmother

and Tom danced in the rain. Simonje gave me a little wooden elephant that he had carved himself. 'Because you tricked him, just like Hare,' he said in such a serious little man's voice that I had to stop myself from laughing.

We were all so happy that I could not bring myself to talk to Magoyela about the incident with Olinji. I had not told Tom either. I was too frightened that he might do something silly to stop Olinji. I tried to put it to the back of my mind but if I hoped that Stepmother might forget too, I was mistaken. Next morning as I went to draw water from the well I sensed someone following me. Although the sun-man had already risen, a chilly dew seemed to fall over me. I quickened my step, but the other person increased speed too.

It was Stepmother. 'My fine young woman,' she called out in a false voice. 'Do not look so worried, my bright-eyed one,' she simpered. 'I have come to help you. Here, give me your container. Today *I* will carry the water.' A forced smile tightened her face like a taut snare.

Having filled our petrol can, she carried it back, talking to me all the way in that deceiving voice of friendship. The stillness of her head, balancing the can, unnerved me. It was poised like a snake's just before it strikes. 'Young woman,' she said, 'Olinji has offered a new *luselo* for you. Having seen your work in the field he is willing to pay even more of a bride price. Olinji is becoming a rich man. Some of his fields were not destroyed by the elephants. You are a very lucky young woman.' I had heard how Olinji had been selling his seeds at greatly inflated prices. All at once Stepmother's voice grew chilled as venom. 'Prepare yourself for marriage. And this time nothing can save you.'

That night I could barely pay attention to the stories that Grandmother told the young ones. Each tale seemed to contain Hyena. And instead of the animal I pictured Olinji with his blunt head, mewling grunts and cruel eyes. How could I spoil the smiles and laughter of Magoyela and the little ones by telling them what Stepmother had said? The planting had gone so well that I had rarely seen Grandmother so happy. I did not have it in me to give her my troubles.

Although Stepmother did not bring Olinji and his stool to me immediately, I knew he was biding his time for the perfect opportunity: a moment when I could not escape. When my father finally came back from the city, Olinji sat with him. Often I would look up and find Olinji's eyes resting on me greedily, like flies sucking the moisture from a child's mouth during the time of want.

'What is the matter, my sister?' Tom asked me one day.

'Nothing, my brother,' I replied.

'Are you sure? Sometimes when the others are laughing, I think you are sad.'

I wanted to tell him everything but I remembered Stepmother's words. Olinji was becoming a powerful person. He was not a good enemy for a young man to make.

The time of want began. The granaries storing last year's harvest ran empty. Even if the generous rains continued then the new maize would not be ready for some time yet. Without the visit of Elephant this would have been a good time. By now we would be enjoying the juicy new cobs and grinding fresh mealie meal. Instead Tom was forced to sell half of the goats so we could afford to buy mealie meal from the district centre. Even then there never seemed to be enough. Yet we still had hope that our new crops would be harvested.

Day after day as Tom grazed the goats and Magoyela and the little ones did chores for Stepmother, Grandmother and I went into the forest to make up the shortfall of our nourishment. We filled many baskets with green caterpillars and roasted them over the fire at night. There were also berries and many edible leaves for us to collect. The harvest of the forest was generous.

Sometimes, however, our foraging brought great danger.

It happened at the termite mounds, those towering,

jagged teeth of red earth. We had piled bundles of dry *bubalubalu* wood round one of the mounds. Usually when we lit the wood, the strong scent of the *bubalubalu* smoke brought out the termites, stunning them so that we were able to collect the grubs for food. But this time no insects came out. Puzzled, I blew the smoke to make it denser. Still nothing emerged. I was just investigating inside the mound when I heard Grandmother speak. 'Mulumbe. Do not move.' The tone of her voice warned me instantly. 'Back away slowly.'

It was only after I had retreated a few paces that I saw the danger. A dark hood of fear fell over my head, blinding me to all else but the large, black snake no more than ten paces away.

The mouth of the snake opened wide as it reared head height from the ground. Black Mamba is the deadliest of all reptiles. The long sibilance of its hiss sickened my blood. Its stiff, forked-tongue probed the air. 'Mulumbe,' Grandmother whispered so as not to startle the snake, 'walk back, child.'

But before I could move. Mamba rushed forward. Now it was only five steps away. I could clearly see the drop of venom beading the needle-sharp fangs. Its head swayed. The tongue flickered, rigid as a finger on the trigger of a gun. At that moment Grandmother stepped in front of me. The hissing flared. The snake loomed a single pace from her. Its nose within a strike of hers. The black body glistened. No one had ever survived Mamba's bite. My breath quickened. Grandmother was sacrificing herself for me . . .

The first thing I knew about my brother's presence was a club flying through the air. Struck full on the head, the venomous reptile lay stunned. Before it could recover, Tom had sprung over and cut off its head with a knife. The long, black, headless body writhed like a dark shadow on the ground. It did not grow still for a long time.

Released, I gulped greedily at the air, laughing and giggling childishly with relief. But Grandmother continued to stare at the still-twitching length of death. When at last she looked up, she was not smiling. 'Take your sister home,' she ordered Tom. 'And be careful. Go straight back to the village. Do not linger here another moment.' And with these abrupt words, she hastened off into the forest alone.

'What is the matter with Grandmother?' I asked Tom as we carried the baskets of food we had foraged back to the village. He did not reply. 'Tom,' I began again, 'where has Grandmother gone?' Still he did not answer. 'What is it?' I persevered. 'I have never seen her like this before.

She still seems worried by the snake.'

'The snake is dead,' Tom replied.

'The way she looked at it –'

'Come on, Mulumbe, it will soon be night.'

I looked up. The sun was blood red as it set. 'Grandmother did not go in the direction of the village.'

'My sister, we must get home.'

'She took a different path.'

'Come on. It is not good to be in the forest at night.'

'Tom,' my voice had dropped to a whisper, 'do you think she has taken the path to the *Sikatonga*?'

'The *Sikatonga*?' he replied suddenly angry. 'Why should she go there?'

The *Sikatonga* lived apart from the rest of the village. Beneath the biggest baobab tree in the forest, his hut stood at the end of a secluded path. If people were ill, or something had happened that they could not explain, they would go to see the *Sikatonga*. I shivered involuntarily at the picture of him sitting on the stool outside his hut motionless as the baobab rising above him. He was an old man, but his eyes were so quick that they seemed to be able to catch your slightest thought.

'My brother,' I said, 'maybe she thinks the *Sikatonga* can help her. Maybe she thinks someone sent that snake as a curse.'

Tom stopped and took my hand. 'Sister, at school I learnt that black mambas live in termite mounds. They only attack if you get between them and their homes. There are no such things as curses. You do not need to believe everything that Grandmother tells you. The fireside is the place for her stories.'

But as the light faded and the growing darkness pressed in on us, it seemed very easy to believe in curses and spells. I thought carefully about what my brother had said. Often Tom would tell me about the things he learnt at school, things that sometimes contradicted what Grandmother said. It was as though there were two separate worlds and I did not know for certain which one I belonged in. 'Ah, Tom,' I said to change the subject, 'should you not have started school by now? I want more English lessons from you.'

His smile faded. 'School will have to wait.'

'What do you mean?'

'My days as a schoolboy are over. At least for now.'

'But you love school.'

'My sister, where will we find the money for school fees? It is going to be hard enough managing just to eat. In fact, tomorrow Peter and I will be leaving you for a while. We are going to another village to help with their harvest. They will give us some mealie meal in exchange.'

'Who will look after your goats?'

'Where do you think we have been getting the money for mealie meal? I have sold the last of the goats already.'

'*All* of them?'

'Every single one.' His face grew troubled. It was hard to think of my brother without picturing the goats or his schoolbooks. 'Mulumbe, hard times are coming. Hunger.'

That night as Grandmother told stories around the campfire, I noticed she wore a necklace of traditional beads. Attached to the necklace was something wrapped in a small pouch. It was a charm against a curse. But what charm could ward off the curse of our growing hunger?

... AND HONEY

And then a fresh catastrophe struck: the rains failed.

My father disappeared to the city again, and Step-mother followed him. The rest of us went to the fields. But no matter how many trips we made to the lake, we could never bring enough water. Slowly but surely the sun burnt our mealie cobs. 'We must never give up,' I ordered, leading the others to the lake time after time. 'Maybe it will rain tomorrow.' But it did not rain the next day, nor the one after that. 'Keep on trying,' I encouraged everyone. 'When Tom comes back he will help us too.' Watched by Fishing Eagle, Grandmother and I carried the largest containers on our heads, followed by Magoyela, then the others, each with their containers in descending size so that even Namaanza waddled behind us with his little gourd of the precious life which is water. It was when Magoyela suddenly collapsed that I realised we had been beaten. Her arms were themselves like the mealie stalks. The task was too much for us. The crops shrivelled to straw.

We returned to the village. Disaster was gathering. Hunger gripped us, and began to squeeze like a python. Now all we could do was harvest the shrinking resources of the forest and wait for Tom to return. The little ones started crying at night. Yet in the midst of all this, one morning, joy visited us. Grandmother and I were foraging in the forest when we heard a loud fluttering of wings. 'Honeyguide!' I cried in delight.

Forgetting our exhaustion, we danced for joy. The little brown bird fluttered and flapped above us. Just then there was a crashing in the undergrowth and Honeybadger plunged across our path. Black and white, with a low, loping gait, he blundered through the forest after the little bird.

'Quick,' said Grandmother.

We followed them through the forest. When we caught up with them, Honeybadger was already halfway up the tree that Honeyguide had led him to. His sharp claws gripped the trunk as he edged higher to where a bees' nest was wedged between two branches. The bird fluttered and sang with mounting excitement. Reaching the nest at last Honeybadger tugged it free with his jaws and carried it down. The enraged bees, thick as a cloud of *bubalubalu* smoke, swarmed over the thief. Their buzzing was like the sound of an approaching storm.

'Ah, Grandmother,' I said, 'Honeybadger must have a thick skin not to feel all those stings.'

'His skin is even thicker than Elephant's,' she returned. 'The bees can sting Honeybadger as many times as there are stars in the sky and he still will not feel a thing.'

Eventually the swarm gave up and flew away. In the silence that followed, the excited chittering of Honeyguide was louder than ever. Honeybadger was already beginning to eat the honey.

Grandmother nudged me. 'Watch him share with Honeyguide.'

And sure enough Honeybadger made room for the bird at the treasure. She perched on a honeycomb beside him and began to peck gratefully.

'Once Honeybadger did not share his honey,' Grandmother whispered. 'So the next time Honeyguide led him to Mamba.'

Concealed behind a tree, watching the partners consuming their sweet feast, my head swirled with anticipation. That morning our breakfast bowls of *nsima* had been little more than watery paste. Our only meal tonight would be what me and Grandmother brought back from the forest. Honeybadger finished first. He lumbered back into the trees licking his chops. When

Honeyguide had flown off at last, I rushed forward. Now it was our turn. 'Here is one sting Honeybadger did not feel!' I cried, holding up a honeycomb that had been dropped on to the ground by Honeybadger. The golden liquid oozed from the waxy comb on to my fingers.

'And here is another,' Grandmother cried – she too was excited. Even the sternest adult becomes a child again when there is honey. 'And another.'

'I have a fourth one, Grandmother!'

'A fifth!'

'A sixth!'

We both began to giggle like children of Namaanza's age. We could never have hoped for such a find. There was more than enough for everyone. 'Mulumbe,' Grandmother said, wrapping each of the combs in a leaf to keep them fresh. 'Bring all my honey babies to me and I will cover them in a blanket!'

And that was not the end of the good news. When we reached the village Tom and Peter were waiting for us. They had brought back sacks of mealie meal and vegetables. We ate until our stomachs were full. And then there was honey.

It was a night of plenty. Around our fire the tears of the little ones became laughter. Each time we placed a bit of the honey on our tongues, a golden sun seemed to rise from deep within, lighting the whole world in an explosion of pure sweetness. Even Magoyela, so quiet since her collapse, appeared to gain new strength.

'Look at me!' shouted Tom leaping up. 'I am Honeyguide. Who will follow?'

The little ones screamed in delight, fluttering their arms as though in excited flight. 'Who will follow, who will follow?'

'I will follow!' cried Peter. 'I am Honeybadger.' And getting down on all fours he lumbered after the others.

'Do not forget the bees!' I laughed, chasing after Peter.

'Look out, Honeybadger,' Grandmother shouted. 'That bee is going to sting you!'

'I don't feel a thing!' Peter laughed back.

'Here come the rest of the hive,' Grandmother added as the buzzing children swarmed all over Peter.

'My hide is thicker than Elephant's!' he cried.

'Peter badger, naughty bees,' said Namaanza, waddling after us.

We all laughed until tears ran down our faces.

When the honey was finished, Grandmother told only the funniest of her countless stories. 'My children, did I ever tell you how Hare got a free ride into the city?'

Eagerly we shook our heads. She stared into the fire.

'Grandmother,' we pleaded, when we could stand

the suspense no longer, 'please tell us.'

'Do you really want to know how he took Baboon's seat on the bus?'

'Yes!'

'Well, I will tell you then. This happened not so long ago, when Mulumbe was about the size of Namaanza. As you know out of all the animals Hare is the only one who has ever been to the city, and he has never forgotten all the strange and wonderful things he saw there. He is forever telling the others about it. They love to listen, especially Baboon. *I wish I could go there too,* Baboon said one day after listening to Hare. *Well you can,* Hare suddenly replied. Baboon shook his head, *Doesn't it cost money to get there?* Hare nodded. *Do you think something so good would cost nothing? But maybe we can still manage it together. My friend, bring your savings, put them with mine and we'll see what we've got.*

'Making sure that no one was watching him Baboon went to the crooked tree where he kept his money. Trembling with excitement he brought his savings to Hare. Hare's lovely long ears twitched at the sight of the money. He could see that there was enough for one ticket to the city and a little spending money besides. *It's not enough to get to the city,* Hare announced as he pretended to add his own money to Baboon's, *but since you are my* friend I will make arrangements. And what's more, I will accompany you. But of course I will let you sit on the special seat. Baboon scratched his head. Special seat? Hare nodded. Why should you sit rubbing shoulders with everyone else in a crowded bus when you're such an important animal? Baboon narrowed his eyes with pleasure, Yes, he said, get me the special seat.

'They set off straight away. Just before they reached the district centre Hare took out a sack. Climb into here, my friend. Baboon's brow knotted with suspicion. Hare smiled knowingly. It's how all the important people are taken to the special seat. His vanity pricked, Baboon climbed inside. Hare tied up the ends. And when we get there, the long-eared one explained, don't worry if you feel yourself flying. It's just the Windi. Baboon was already feeling hot in the sack. The Windi? he demanded irritatedly. Yes, said Hare, he's the one in charge of throwing luggage on top of the bus . . . I mean, making sure the important people get their special seats.

'At last they arrived at the bus stop. What have you got in that sack? The Windi asked Hare. Just some wooden stools I'm selling in the city, the clever one replied, and doing his job the Windi threw the sack on to the top of the bus with all the rest of the luggage. The bus set off.

'Inside the sack Baboon was bounced and shaken until

he was quite disorientated. *I don't think much of these special seats,* he thought to himself, *if this is what it's like for the important people then I hate to think what poor Hare must be putting up with.* The thought cheered him up. Little did he know that at that very moment Hare was stretching his legs comfortably across the nice wide aisle of the bus eating a juicy mango he had bought from another passenger with Baboon's money.

'After a while the *Windi* came down the vehicle. *Tickets, please,* he called. *One please,* Hare said, once again taking out Baboon's money. *Tickets, please,* the *Windi* continued along the aisle. *Hey,* an invisible voice suddenly shouted, *surely those in the special seats should have a ticket to hold?* The *Windi* looked about, *Who said that?* he demanded. *I did,* the invisible voice continued. *An important person in a special seat.* The bus screeched to a halt. Terrified the driver and the *Windi* searched their vehicle for the mysterious speaker. *Why have we stopped?* Baboon demanded. *It's coming from the roof,* the driver whispered to the Windi. They went outside; Baboon was complaining at the top of his voice, *When you get a special seat the least you expect is a ticket.* As quietly as he could the *Windi* climbed up on to the roof and hurled the talking sack as far away as he could. The bus drove off at top speed. Buying another mango,

Hare settled down for a comfortable journey . . .'

As I sat round the fire listening to Grandmother, my heart swelled inside me as though to the size of the moon-woman's face staring down on us. The honey had brought happiness back. I wanted it to last forever. Even the firelight seemed to be laughing as it flickered over our faces. After Grandmother's stories, Tom and Peter danced for us, showing us how they had brought in the harvest for the other village. They leapt higher and higher until it seemed they were dancing with the moon-woman herself.

HARE AND HYENA

The mealie meal and vegetables Tom and Peter had brought back soon ran out. We grew hungrier and hungrier. Even the mice and little birds that we trapped were growing scarce. One night little Namaanza began to moan. I lay in the darkness beside Grandmother listening. We could do nothing to ease him. Every night he moaned, and every night his moaning grew a little quieter until you could only hear him when your ear was pressed to his face. His breathing began to rattle as though he were a gourd maraca with a single seed left to shake. And when he shook it, I knew that I was listening to the sound of approaching famine.

Like little Kapu, Namaanza's life was also cut short. Where once he had laughed and played, he left behind silence: a slow, smothering silence in which the flies liked to land. We buried him in the cruel, red earth; so tiny a body. Tom led us in our funeral song: 'Please tell us what we have done to deserve this?' But I could not sing. And

I did not dare let myself cry. The tears that Grandmother had said were good welled within me like a rising river. If I let them flow they threatened to drown everything. I said goodbye to Namaanza as I had said goodbye to Kapu, but this time I made a promise. I promised the two little boys that had been taken away from us that I would do everything I could to save those left behind. I had made my promise. But how would I be able to keep it?

Father and Stepmother did not come back from the city. They missed the funeral.

A week later I saw a vulture slowly circling above the village. Grandmother's words sprang into my mind. *Already the vulture is circling. Before the rains return, he will find my bones.* Tom and Peter left the village again. There was a rumour that drought-relief maize was being given out at the district centre. The failing of the rains meant that all the villages were hungry now. We waited many days for the boys to return, but still they did not come back with any food. There was not a single thing left to eat. How would I be able to keep my promise to Namaanza and Kapu?

'Mulumbe,' Grandmother whispered, waking me tenderly one morning before dawn, 'today we are going to have to ask the forest to give up its deepest secrets.'

'Secrets, Grandmother?'

'We are going to have to ask her to share them with us. But I do not know what she will say.'

The sun-man was rising as we walked along the path that took us deep into the forest. The dawn revealed a barren place. Everything had been picked bare: all the fruit, all the edible leaves and insects. No hornbills came to watch us. The sunbirds did not sing. The silence was as strange and dry as the forest. It was as though a great fire had destroyed everything.

'I have a riddle for you, Mulumbe,' Grandmother said.

Although my heart was heavy I tried to sound enthusiastic. 'Ah, is it a good one?'

'It *is* a good one, but it is also sad. I am the clothes that have been burnt, and only the belt is left. Who am I?'

As we walked along I searched for the solution. Many of the trees had even had their bark stripped. The path, stretching ahead and behind, seemed naked, unprotected. 'Grandmother, I have found the answer to the riddle.'

'Tell me who I am then, girl.'

'You are the forest. All the leaves, berries and small animals have been taken, only the path is left. The clothes have been burnt, the belt alone remains.'

She nodded and smiled sadly. 'Everything that the eye can see has been gathered. Only what is hidden is left.

Mulumbe, today the forest must share her secrets. Today she must tell us where she keeps her famine foods. You see, child, the earth has many secret roots and berries. They are hard to find. Most people have even forgotten where to look. They are bitter to eat, but they give some nourishment. You must handle them carefully. Some of them will make you very ill unless you know exactly how to cook them. Mulumbe, many of them can kill you.'

'Is that why some of our people have been ill?'

Grandmother nodded. 'Even if they can find them, they have forgotten the old ways of preparing them. If you do not boil them in the pot long enough they are poisonous.' Suddenly she grew very serious. 'Mulumbe, you must treat the forest's secrets with respect.'

I looked at Grandmother. She was so thin. Ever since we had lost our crops to Elephant she had been sustaining the whole family. I often saw her giving her share of the watery *nsima* to us children. In fact, I could not remember the last time I saw her eat.

As we went in search of these secrets my empty stomach felt like a drum being beaten by the merciless hands of hunger. Just to walk was exhausting. Some people in the village had already given up. They lay outside their huts, waiting. But waiting for what?

I was just beginning to wonder how far we had to search

when Grandmother fell to her knees. She laid her head flat against the ground as though listening. Seeming to hear something she took up her little wooden spade. Deeper and deeper she dug until reaching her arm down into the hole she caught hold of something and began to pull. It was only after a long and difficult struggle that I heard something snap free. A shrivelled tuber lay on the ground. 'You must cook this for two full days,' Grandmother said. 'Or it will kill you in less time than it takes to boil the water in the pot.' The tuber looked like a finger that had been pulled from a great hand buried deep in the earth.

For many days Grandmother and I probed into the very womb of the earth, finding what seemed only the smallest of things after the greatest of efforts. One late afternoon as we walked home, weary and stumbling, I looked up. The sky was full of vultures. Their shadows crossed our path.

In the hut that night Grandmother's breathing was different. Towards dawn it became congested as though a blanket of thorns had been pulled over her face. 'What is the matter, Grandmother?'

She did not answer.

'Can you get up?'

'I do not think so, Mulumbe.'

A great numbness came over me. I did not know what to do.

At last Grandmother spoke again. 'Mulumbe?'

'Yes, Grandmother?' Her voice sounded far away, as though she was standing outside the hut and speaking to me through the mud and daub.

'*You* must feed everyone now.'

'Me?'

'The forest has decided to share her secrets with you.'

'You will be all right, Grandmother,' I said, forcing my tone to sound bright. 'Soon Tom will come back with mealie meal from the district centre and you will get up. Together we will gather more famine foods. Tomorrow you will . . .'

'Tomorrow is a river I will never cross.'

I tried to comfort her, but I choked on the words, as though I had swallowed a bone.

'And now, child, go and make sure your famine food is ready. The little ones are hungry.'

The meal was made from the beans of the *musweezyo*. They were very bitter, but the children ate hungrily. When I brought Grandmother's bowl into the hut however, she would not touch it. I lifted the spoon to her lips. Her mouth would not open. I tried again and again. She did not take a single spoonful. Sitting in the half-light of the hut, I ate my famine porridge in silence.

I had finished eating when a blur of movement in the

rafters above caught my eye. Snatching up a sharpened stick I speared the lizard. Perhaps Grandmother would eat some meat. Cutting off its poisonous tail, I boiled it. But still she would not eat.

Outside, countless children had gathered. They had heard that I had caught a lizard. All the mice and rats had long since been eaten. Nobody in the village had tasted meat for a long, long time. At that moment I would have given my life to feed them all. But the lizard gave only half a mouthful for my own little brothers and sisters. 'What about you, Mulumbe?' Magoyela asked.

'I have eaten my bit already,' I lied.

I watched Luuwo swallow her meat. Her eyes closed in the terrible pleasure of her hunger being relieved for just an instant. I had to look away.

'Who is that?' Grandmother whispered when I returned. Her voice sounded even further away as though she stood on the far bank of a river.

'It is Mulumbe.'

'Mulumbe?'

'Yes, Grandmother.'

'I thought for a moment that you were –' She broke off in confusion. 'Mulumbe, I thought you were my Grandfather, coming to take me for a walk by the river.'

I could feel something rustling feebly towards me in

the half-light of the hut. It was her hand looking for mine. She found it. Her grip was weak. It was as though I was holding the hand of a little girl. A film now covered her eyes. She had gone blind. Softly, almost too softly for me to hear, she began to sing. 'Mulumbe, is a special girl.' Her voice was jerky, her breath uneven. 'In her, the ancestors return. In her, the river flows again. She is as beautiful as the *kadondwe* cormorant. If you ask me who is this walking along the riverbank with me, I will tell you it is Mulumbe, the special one.' Breaking off her singing, she drew me close. 'I have something to tell you, child.'

I bent right over her so that her breath tickled my ear. 'What is it, Grandmother?'

'Mulumbe,' she smiled. 'My Mulumbe. When you were born I told them to call you Mulumbe. Do you know what your name means?'

'Mulumbe means a message,' I replied.

She nodded. 'You are a message. And a messenger too. You are the keeper of the story. You are the restorer of justice. Child, you are the river. Never let them dam you.'

'I do not understand, Grandmother,' I whispered. 'I do not understand anything of what you say.'

But her eyes showed no sign of having heard me. She seemed to be drawing on her last remaining strength. 'Mulumbe, I have one last riddle for you.' The old

woman tried to raise herself but managed only to lift her head a little. I stared at her unseeing eyes. They were deeper than the lake itself and they held everything that I loved. The whole world seemed to be contained in them. Although blind now, she still pretended to scan the rafters of the hut as though searching for a riddle as we always did. 'Ah,' she smiled. 'I have found one.'

'Is it a good one?' I murmured, hardly able to trust my voice.

She nodded. 'It is a good one. Are you ready?'

'I am ready.'

'I am a cloud, I can blow anywhere.'

'I am a cloud?'

'I am a cloud, I can blow anywhere. Who am I?'

Before I had the chance to begin working the riddle out, Grandmother fell back. The soft, but troubled tangle of breathing rustling against my neck told me that she had fallen asleep.

Emerging from the hut, the bright sunlight struck me like a blow. I staggered under the impact. When I had caught my balance I saw Stepmother glaring at me, fiercer than even the cruel man in the sun. I did not know she had come back from the city. 'What are you doing, lazy one?'

'Grandmother is ill,' I managed to say.

'Good. That will mean more food for the rest of us. Go and get me something to eat. I have been travelling all night.'

Before I could stop myself my anger throbbed out: 'Don't you talk about Grandmother like that!'

'How dare you answer me back?' Stepmother spat. A terrible smile sharpened her face like a knife. I had never seen her look crueller than at that moment. 'It is better she dies sooner rather than later. There is no point playing on a broken drum. As your punishment I forbid you to give the old one any more food. And remember, when she is gone there will be no one to protect you. Now, go and get some food for me.'

'No!'

'What? You will do as I say. I am in charge now. Not that dried stick. Come back. Come back. Just wait until I catch you . . .'

I hurried along the path that led to the *Sikatonga*. The closer I got, the more I wanted to turn and run. But there was nowhere left for me to go. Stepmother would be looking for me. No one had ever defied her like that before. But I did not care. All I wanted to do was to help Grandmother.

At last the sacred tree loomed out of the forest like a

giant. The baobab's trunk was wider than Elephant, but its branches were as spindly as that great beast's tail. Underneath stood the hut, the oldest and largest in the village. The thick wooden walls and brooding roof blazed with ochre, red as the setting sun. Deep as night, the dark hole of its door-opening seemed to lead to another world. Human-like shapes encircled the *Sikatonga*'s hut: straw shrines to the ancestors. As I approached, they seemed to be staring at me.

A breeze blew as though from nowhere and the air was filled with a strange whispering of many voices. The hair on the back of my neck crackled like twigs tossed on the fire. The voices rose and fell. People seemed to be calling to me from the shrines. 'Who are you?' I stammered. The wind blew even more strongly and the voices clamoured. I was just about to run when I saw that the branches of the sacred tree were filled with charms chiming in the wind.

But the croaky voice that suddenly spoke from the depths of the hut was definitely human. 'Who are you?' it demanded.

I curtseyed to the door-opening. It was the *Sikatonga*. '*Sikatonga* Sir, my name is Mulumbe Mudenda.'

'Why does Mulumbe Mudenda disturb the sleep of the spirits in the shrine?'

'She has come for help.'

There was no reply. I stared at the hut's dark mouth, but could see nothing.

'Come closer, girl,' the *Sikatonga* suddenly said.

I edged my way through the circle of straw figures.

'Now tell me what help you want.'

'I seek the *Sikatonga*'s help, Sir.'

'And why should the *Sikatonga* help?'

Although my mind was racing, I tried to remember the traditional words. 'Because he is the Steward of the Earth.'

'The Steward of the Earth?' His voice echoed bitterly in the hut. 'A poor, thin earth.'

'Will you help me, Sir?'

'Everybody wants help these days. But there is so little that I can do. What can a mouse do to stop a charging lion?'

When the *Sikatonga* finally stepped out into the light, the air between us seemed to swirl. I stepped back. It was as though a great vulture with wide black wings had emerged from the hut's dark stomach.

'My child, do not be afraid.' The gentleness of his words shocked me. His face was not unkind. 'I know you, Mulumbe Mudenda. I have been watching you.'

His hair was white. His skin blotched with lighter

patches that gave him a strange, mottled look, like a snake that has half cast off its skin. His old body was malnourished.

'Yes,' he continued. 'I have seen you in the forest with your Grandmother. She and I have spoken about you.'

'*Sikatonga,* it is because of her that I come to the Steward of the Earth.'

He held out a bowl. 'Come here, Mulumbe.' I hesitated. 'What are you frightened of, girl?'

'Nothing, Sir,' I managed to reply although my heart beat like the hooves of a stampeding buffalo herd. The straw shrines seemed to shuffle towards me.

'Then take it, girl. And drink.'

One hand supported at the wrist by the other, I took the bowl. But I could not bring myself to drink.

'Do you think I might harm you?'

'No, Sir.'

'Do you fear a curse in the drink?'

His gaze grew piercing for a moment, then lost its fire. 'It is only *mutumu* bark mixed with water. It will give you a little strength.'

I felt his eyes boring into me as I drank, but not in the same way that Olinji stared at me. It did not make me feel like prey being stalked by predator. Instead I was filled with hope that he might not only be able to help

Grandmother but that he might be able to help me keep my promise to Namaanza. And perhaps he could assist me with Olinji. But before I could say anything he had turned away.

He bent down and picked up four sticks from the beaten earth by his fire. Strange, beautiful patterns decorated the wood. Lifting his arm, he tossed them into the air. The patterns disappeared in a swirl, only to reappear again as the sticks landed. Looking at them, the *Sikatonga* sighed. 'There is nothing I can do,' he whispered.

A hornbill flew into the spindly branches of the baobab. But it did not call. After a few moments it flew on, taking with it my hope that this old, deflated man might be able to change the course of events. 'Nothing has been right since the great flood covered the graves of our ancestors,' the *Sikatonga* said in a thin voice. 'The ancestors have been disturbed and they wander. The shades cannot rest. Nothing can be right until they wander no more.'

I have never felt so alone as I did walking back along the path to the village. Stepmother would be waiting for me and there seemed nothing that I could do to help Grandmother. The first huts of the village were coming into view when I suddenly stopped. What about the clinic

at the district centre? Perhaps a doctor could help. Tom would be there too; surely he would know what to do. It was a long way. But I set off immediately.

I had not gone very far when I realised that I was being followed. I quickened my pace. But whatever it was kept up with me. Calling on all my reserves of strength I ran. But each time I stopped to listen, over the thud of my heart came the continuing tread of a pursuer. I had forgotten about the men who took my mother away.

Then I found that the path ahead was blocked. An old tree trunk had fallen across it. Coming to a halt, I stared at it helplessly. I did not have the strength to climb over it. In fact, I didn't have any strength left at all. The running had exhausted me. Neither could I fly like Fishing Eagle. The trunk was hollow. I crawled inside, pushing myself in as far as possible, trusting that there was no snake or troublesome spider lurking there. I picked up a sharp pointed branch. If an animal was after me then at least I could strike. Holding my breath I waited.

As my hunter approached the fallen tree, I listened with every fibre of my being. It was making too much noise to be Leopard. Neither had I heard the blood-freezing growl that advertises the presence of Lion. It had been very slow in the chase. Perhaps it was an injured hyena. Injured animals are always the most

dangerous. They get the taste for human flesh.

The pursuer reached the tree. It stopped. My grip tightened on the stick. I pictured an injured hyena, sniffing the air, puzzled by the sudden disappearance of its prey. Suddenly there was a loud crunch from the tree: the injured hyena had jumped on to the trunk. The whole tree groaned under its weight.

But it wasn't Hyena. Nor was it the men who took my mother. I squinted up through a hole in the tree trunk to see Olinji sitting there above me. 'I know you are in there,' he growled.

I did not reply.

'Come out, girl.'

I kept quiet.

'This time there is no one else here, just you and me. That old fool can't meddle. Why not come out and have a little chat?' His laughter was a gurgling grunt.

I stared at him through the tiny hole. He was sitting on the trunk, very pleased with himself. His rotten teeth were twisted into a self-satisfied leer.

'Come out now, girl,' he commanded.

'Should Hare come out when Hyena asks?' The words had left my mouth without me even thinking.

His red-rimmed eyes bulged angrily. Then I could see him relax. He knew he was master of the situation. 'Hare

should come out when Hyena has something that he wants to share.'

'Hyena never shares with Hare,' I returned.

He laughed again as though to humour me. 'Sometimes Hyena is in a good mood.'

'Even Hyena's good moods are not to be trusted.'

This was too much for him. 'Enough of this stupid talk, girl.' All at once his voice boomed inside the trunk and my nostrils were filled with the acrid stench of sour beer and cruelty: the musk of a predator without the smallest shred of pity for its prey. He was crawling up the tree trunk towards me.

It all happened very quickly. His fingers clutched at me, I kicked them away. Bellowing he hurled himself up the narrowing space. But his body wedged tight. Unable to get closer, his hands lunged repeatedly, his long fingernails stinging my ankles like scorpions.

Screaming with frustration, swearing and cursing, he corkscrewed his way back to daylight. The tree groaned as he sat on it again. 'You will have to come out eventually,' he growled. 'I will get you then. I don't care how long I have to wait.'

In the darkness of my precarious hiding place I pictured Grandmother lying in her hut. I could not just stay here. I had to get to the district centre, but *how*? I stared down the

trunk for inspiration, but saw only the daylight. All I could hear was Olinji's breathing above me. I was trapped.

Then something began to happen. Slowly, the light at the entrance to the hollow tree was thickening. It began to flicker and dance like flames. And all at once I seemed to be sitting again round the fire listening to Grandmother's stories. *Mulumbe, do you remember what Hare did when he was trapped in a log?*

The plan formed itself quickly. I only needed the nerve to carry it out. 'Olinji?' I called out.

He grunted in reply.

'Olinji?' I persevered. 'Have you agreed a good *luselo* or have you too become a poor man like all the rest of the village?'

'Me like the rest?' He scoffed arrogantly. 'I have some fields right beside the lake. They have not been lost to the drought.'

'Ah, you must be an important person.'

'Yes, I am.'

'So it must be a good *luselo.*'

He laughed to himself. 'It's the best one you could get.'

'I thought it was. I just wanted to check.'

'When others go hungry, Olinji gorges himself.'

I took a deep breath. 'Yes,' I said. 'All the women *do* say that Olinji is the finest man.'

'They do?'

At that moment I pretended to begin weeping and moaning like Hare in the log. 'Oh, please forgive me! *Please* forgive me for what happened at the fields. I just could not believe that such an important man like you would want me.'

'Heh, heh, heh. I am important, aren't I?'

'And please forgive me for what I am doing now.'

'What are you doing now?'

'You will laugh at me, Oh Olinji, most important man in the village.'

His brow lowered suspiciously. 'Tell me.'

'Well, you must know that a mere girl like me cannot look at an important man like you. That would be disrespectful and rude. But since everybody has said how handsome you are, I have thought of nothing else but getting to look at you. That is why I brought you here.'

'It is?'

'I knew that this tree trunk was here. And that in it there is a hole. I thought that if I got you up on the trunk then I could look at you closely through my hole.'

I watched him searching the trunk for the hole. When he located it, all at once we found ourselves eye to eye. 'You know that I am going to beat you as soon as I get hold of you, don't you?' he growled.

'I don't care, I just want to see you for myself.'

'You can see me now.'

'Come a little closer.'

He shifted over the trunk and craned his head down.

'Closer, closer,' I begged, even though the rancid stench of his breath was like a snake wrapping itself round my throat.

Olinji lowered a bloodshot eye right over the hole. With all my strength, I jabbed up the stick. His dreadful, raging shouts were still echoing through the forest as I slipped from the trunk and bounded away. By the time he had stopped screaming, I was long gone.

DROUGHT-RELIEF

In each of the thinly scattered villages I passed, people sat motionless outside their huts. Only the flies seemed to be moving. And me. I *had* to save Grandmother. The thought of her gave me the strength to keep on going.

It was late afternoon by the time I arrived at the district centre.

When I had come here with my father there had been a thriving market place full of people buying and selling. Now there were no stalls, no pots of bubbling food, no dried fish and no vegetables. The place was silent, deserted. I was just wondering what to do when – between two of the low buildings, the church and the school – I caught sight of a large queue. Somebody was waving at me from it.

'Mulumbe, Mulumbe!'

'My brother!'

It was Tom. When I went over I saw that he was with Peter. '*Wayusa, biyeni*, Mulumbe,' Peter greeted me.

In the midst of my own pain, I remembered his. Mutinta had not come out of her hut for such a long time. '*Iyii*, Peter.'

The queue snaked past the doors of All Souls Church and then passed out of sight. Never before had I seen so many people together. And none of them was making a sound. This great mass of countless individuals might have just been one sad, silent person. 'What are they all doing here?' I asked in amazement.

'The same as us,' Peter explained. 'Every day people say there is going to be a drought-relief delivery. We wait. But it does not come. Maybe it will be tomorrow.'

'My sister, what are you doing here?' Tom asked.

I tried to answer, but exhaustion and hunger had caught up with me. I would have fallen if Peter had not taken hold of me. When I came round, Tom was gently sitting me down in the shade cast by the church. 'Drink this,' he said, giving me some water. 'And then eat a little.' He held out something wrapped in a leaf.

It was a piece of fish. 'Oh, my brother,' I whispered. 'You know it is illegal to fish in the lake without a licence. You could go to prison.'

'My sister, so how are we to feed ourselves?' He showed me a bag. It was full of dried fish.

Before I had time to think twice, the food was in

my mouth. It was the first time I had eaten with no regard for the other members of my family. 'Do not worry,' urged Tom, as though sensing my guilt. 'We will soon be carrying the fish *and* a sack of mealie meal home. We need our strength to be able to do that.' He waited patiently for me to finish eating before asking again: 'My sister, why are you here?'

'Ah, Tom, there is bad news at home.'

He stiffened. 'The marauders have come back?'

'No. It is Grandmother.'

'Grandmother?'

'She is sick.'

His voice was very small. 'How sick?'

'My brother, she cannot get up. I think . . .'

'What do you think, Mulumbe?'

'That unless we help her, she may never get up again.'

'She is that bad?'

'Yes. That is why I have come here,' I continued. 'I thought that someone in the clinic might be able to help her.'

'The clinic?'

'Yes. A doctor. Tom, where is the doctor who will help her?'

He bowed his head. 'Mulumbe, the clinic will not be able to help Grandmother.' And getting up, he went back to the queue and sat down once more.

My legs felt a little unsteady but I tottered after him. 'What do you mean? The clinic is there to help people.' But he did not answer; he was buried too deep in his sorrow. When I explained the situation to Peter, he shook his head.

'The clinic cannot help your Grandmother,' he said.

'Why not?' I demanded, suddenly angry.

He lifted his hands in a gesture of despair.

Tears blistered my eyes. 'I don't believe you!' I shouted. Those in the queue around us looked over. Girls were not supposed to shout like this. 'If you two won't help me then I'll find the clinic by myself.'

'Mulumbe,' Peter replied, 'let me show you the clinic.'

We walked down a dusty road to a flat roofed, one-storey building. He pointed to an even longer queue waiting here. It too was silent. Everywhere, it seemed people had lost their voices.

'Mulumbe, look, they have all come for help too.'

The suffering could only be seen in their eyes and the occasional sigh of pain that blew through them like a breeze troubling the tips of elephant grass. Their few possessions were gathered around them. The ground had been charred by cooking fires. It was clear that theirs was a long wait. From somewhere in the middle of the waiting

throng a newborn baby gave its first cry of life. But the baby quickly fell silent too, as though realising that crying would do little good in the hungry world it found itself in.

'They wait day after day,' Peter said. 'How many people can one doctor see? Anyway, Mulumbe, even if there was some medicine, how could you pay for it?'

'Pay?'

'The government no longer gives medical help.'

A great weight of sorrow fell on my back. I had made a wasted journey. And all the while Grandmother was dying. We walked back to Tom in silence. He was still sitting in the queue. 'My brother,' I said to him, 'I will see you at home.'

Tom's eyes were filled with tears. 'My sister, you can not travel all that way now. You must rest first.'

'But Grandmother is waiting for me . . .'

Peter shook his head. 'Mulumbe, you are exhausted. You would never make it.' And you should *never* travel alone at night.'

And all at once the words of Grandmother's riddle sprang into my mouth. 'I am a cloud, I can blow anywhere.'

'What do you mean?' Peter asked.

'I do not know.'

In the distance there was a sudden rumbling as of

approaching thunder. It grew louder. Tom jumped to his feet. The silent queue seethed into life as people began to wave and yell. A lorry was lumbering slowly towards us.

Already bodies were swarming over the vehicle. When they fell off, they just jumped back on. And still the lorry trundled forward heavily, like a Honeybadger surrounded by bees.

'The relief is here,' Peter shouted in excitement.

'Maybe all is not lost.'

When the rains arrive suddenly the dry streambed near our village becomes a rushing torrent. Everything in its path is swept aside. The drought-relief queue now became a human torrent. The long, long patience of many days foamed into a whirring mass of elbows and hands as the starving people clawed towards the back of the lorry.

'Keep back, Mulumbe!' Tom suddenly shouted over. 'On the last delivery someone was crushed to death. And here, take the fish.'

I stepped to one side just in time to avoid the lorry. Utterly surrounded, it could go no further. Bare hands ripped the tarpaulin off its back and the drivers looked on helplessly as people threw themselves at the white sacks of mealie meal. If it had been like a torrent of floodwater before, now it was a fire. A raging fire with leaping flames of fists and elbows, and feet and teeth. The old and young

were crushed. A few had sticks and were trying to beat their way to the front of the queue. Even the usually gentle Peter was fighting a path to the lorry, while Tom, head down, was digging himself there like a spade biting through soil.

It was like a frenzy of skeletons.

'Come on, Mulumbe!' A sack bulging on his back, Tom tore himself free from the crowd. Peter was there too, similarly laden. 'My sister,' said Tom, 'we learnt at school that most of our illnesses come from malnutrition. There are vitamin packs in with the mealie meal. Once she has eaten well Grandmother will get better. Everyone will get better. Let's go home.'

'Should I go and get another sack?' I asked.

'You would be ripped to pieces. You bring the fish. Now come on. There is no time to waste.'

News of the delivery of the drought-relief was spreading quickly. As we left the district centre, the paths were thronged with hurrying people, desperate to reach the lorry before its precious cargo ran out.

We did not go back the way I had come.

'We'll take the quieter ways,' Peter explained. 'When people are hungry it is not a good idea to walk past their villages with food.'

But we had not gone far before I began struggling to

keep up. 'Hare,' I whispered, 'lend me your long legs just until I reach home.' I ground my teeth and tried to keep up. But still I fell behind. The others had to wait for me. 'We will sleep here,' Tom announced.

'But we must get home, my brother.'

'My sister, you are too tired.'

'But Grandmother –'

'Will you help Grandmother by killing yourself?'

'Tom is right,' said Peter. 'We all need rest. The sacks are heavy. Besides soon it will be dark.'

Nodding, I closed my eyes. I could not take another step. Throwing myself to the ground I felt like sleeping immediately. 'Go on then, Hare,' I whispered under my breath. 'Take back your legs and run home. Tell Grandmother we are coming tomorrow. Tell her not to give up until tomorrow.'

The boys made a shelter – some branches roofing a frame of poles. We lit a fire and ate some fish. The circle of light made by the flames seemed broken without Grandmother. 'Do you think she will be all right?' I asked Tom.

'You will see. Mulumbe, as soon as we can just get these sacks home, then everything will be all right. There is the fish too. Everyone will be able to eat now. Everyone will get stronger. Even the littlest ones.'

As the night deepened I thought of my promise to Namaanza and Kapu. Nobody felt like talking. The only stories being told were those croaked by the night frogs, and I could not understand them.

'My sister,' Tom said at last, 'Peter and I have come to a decision. We are going away.'

'Going away?'

'Mulumbe, we are going to the mines.'

'You can't!' The coal mines were deep beneath the red earth. Three days' walk from the village, they felt so distant as to seem to be over the edge of the world. Many who went down them were injured. Some did not even return, like Peter's father who had lost his life in a terrible disaster a mile under the ground.

'Mulumbe,' said Peter gently, 'we have no other choice. I must look after my brothers and sisters.' He looked at Tom. 'Mutinta still will not leave the hut. I have no father to earn money.'

'Our father is dead as well,' said Tom. 'At least, dead to us.'

I did not know what to say. My brother's voice was hard. 'But, Tom, will you *ever* go back to school?'

Peter sighed. 'If we do not go to the mines then what will people eat once the fish and this sack of mealie meal is empty?'

'You cannot give up on school.'

'School is for people with full bellies,' said Tom.

I fell silent. A girl has no say in such matters. 'When are you going?'

'At the end of the month,' Tom replied. 'We have already registered our names.'

As we stretched out to sleep I gazed up at the stars through the makeshift ceiling of branches. I felt as though I was lying lost at the bottom of a deep mine staring up at the lights of those searching for me. That night I dreamt that no one could find me, no matter how hard they looked.

When I woke the next morning, the sun was just beginning to rise. The two boys were sleeping contentedly. After their long ordeal at the district centre I did not bother to wake them, but crept away to collect firewood. They had been right. We would have to be fully rested and eat a good breakfast if we were going to be able to carry the heavy sacks home.

It was a beautiful morning and the dew soothed my feet as the sun opened like a flower. Searching in the special wombs and pouches of the earth as Grandmother had taught me, I found some berries and edible grubs. Tom was right: Grandmother would surely get better.

It was the sudden shriek of a hornbill that brought me to a stop. I looked up from the bush where I had been foraging. The colour of the sun pouring through the forest canopy showed me that the morning was advancing. The boys had slept long enough. It was time for us to get back to Grandmother.

But I could not find them. I walked back the way I thought I had come and did not reach the camp. I changed directions but still could not find the others.

Suddenly I heard some voices. They were cold, hostile and bullying. Fear sprang into the pit of my stomach, as though I had swallowed a frog. I braced myself for flight. The forest could hide me from the danger. But first I had to warn Tom and Peter.

I crawled towards the voices. Through the intervening forest foliage, I could make out four or five men. They were standing by our shelter. Without realising it, I had traced a complete circle through the forest and come back to the camp. A talon of sweat traced my spine. I crept forward. Suddenly I froze. The voices belonged to the night marauders. And they were forcing my brother to his knees.

Lion would have charged with open jaws and a roar. Baboon might have tried swinging through the trees and plucking my brother to safety. But being just a girl, what could I possibly do?

'I have no food,' Tom was saying to the men.

'We know you've been to collect it from the drought-relief lorry,' one of the marauders snapped in reply. His accent was strange. He was not used to speaking our language. He talked as though he was chewing the bitter *mululwe* leaf.

'I have no food,' Tom repeated.

'Say *Sir* when you speak to us,' another one of the marauders commanded, his voice too was strange and sour. 'Now tell us where your food is.'

'I have no food . . .' Tom's face twitched slightly before he added: 'Sir.'

A third marauder advanced towards my brother. A cold shudder gripped my spine like the jaws of a hyena. He was holding a gun. 'Is it true what they say about you lake people?' he demanded. 'I have heard that you have six toes.' The others burst into mocking laughter.

'Sir,' Tom replied, I could hear him struggling to keep his voice calm. Despite the danger, he could not let this cruel insult pass. 'How can you believe stories like that? Do you not know that God gives all human beings five toes? Or did you not go to school?'

The man with the gun grunted dangerously and stepped closer to my brother. He seemed just about to fire

at Tom when his comrades restrained him. 'Get him to feed us first,' they told him.

Reluctantly he agreed. 'And then,' he said, lowering the barrel of his weapon so that it was almost touching Tom's foot, 'I'll count each toe with a bullet. Now, where is your food?'

I looked about desperately. There was no sight of Peter. I could not see the sacks either. 'I told you, I have no food, Sir,' Tom said.

But in answering he had glanced at a thicket of tall grass. One of the marauders went over and reached into the grass. He hauled out one of our sacks. The others whooped with laughter. 'Light a fire,' said the man with the gun. 'And cook us some of your lovely *nsima*, Six Toes.'

My mouth ran dry. Numb with terror I closed my eyes. Kapu, Namaanza, Grandmother, Tom: I had failed them all.

It was at this moment of darkness that once again Grandmother's voice seemed to reach me. *Mulumbe*, she whispered, *do you remember the time when Hare was trapped by Lion, Baboon and Hyena?*

'I remember,' I whispered. 'Lion and Hyena had locked their jaws on his leg.'

And as though I was listening to it at that very

moment I pictured the tale. I could even hear Baboon asking whether they should cook him in oil or boil him in water, but little did they know that Hare was both a clever ventriloquist and a perfect mimic. Without his captors realising, he spoke in Baboon's voice, *You two, why are you biting that tree root? Drop it. Quick*, this *one is Hare's leg. The hairy one.* Instantly Lion and Hyena set Hare free and sunk their teeth into Baboon's leg. *Owww!* Baboon screeched as Hare bounded away to freedom.

But instead of hope, this story brought me only despair. Unlike Hare I was not a clever mimic nor a ventriloquist. How could I make others hear what I wanted them to hear?

It was a Y-shaped stick lying on the ground at my feet that gave me the idea. With the elastic from my skirt waistband, it made the perfect catapult. Now all I needed was a stone. I could see a pile close to the marauders. How could I reach it without being noticed? Creeping like Civet Cat through the scrub, I edged towards the stones. No more than the length of two tree trunks from my brother, I bent down and picked one up.

The marauders were mocking Tom as he lit a fire for them. 'You will make someone a lovely wife.'

There was still no sign of Peter. Fitting the stone to the elastic, my hand shook; but as I peered above the

tangle of vegetation to take aim, both Hare and Grandmother seemed to be standing behind me holding the catapult steady. The instant I fired, I brought my foot sharply down on a stick. A loud crack rang out just as the stone crashed into branches of a tree close to the marauders.

'Gunfire!' the marauders shouted, scattering and hurling themselves to the ground.

In these moments of confusion, Tom ran.

The marauder with the gun was the first to recover. He looked up and lifted the weapon to his shoulder. But before he could take aim I fired again. It was at that moment I recognised him. He was the one who had taken my mother.

The stone missed him, but hit his gun. Yelping in shock, he dropped it, and raised his hands like Baboon who lifts a rock in search of a tasty grub but finds a coiled snake. By the time he snatched up his weapon again, Tom had slipped into the forest.

But I had not hidden myself. I was kneeling there with my catapult for all to see. With a roar of rage the gunman charged. I plunged into the forest. It was going to be a chase to the death. A crack of lightning struck the trees above me. He was firing.

A DRY, WHITE SEASON

When I was unable to run any further I threw myself on the ground. My heart seemed to be bursting from my chest like a flock of *quelea* birds exploding from a field of millet. It took a long time before their wing beats began to slow.

I had not got my breath back fully when I felt vibrations on the earth all around where I lay. I did not need to look up to know that somebody was standing over me. So, they had caught me. There would be no use begging. My mother had begged and still they had taken her.

The marauder stood there silently like a rhinoceros pawing the ground before he charges. I waited to be crushed underfoot.

'Mulumbe. Oh, Mulumbe!'

I looked up in disbelief. 'Peter!'

His teeth were chattering with fear. 'Mulumbe, I thought you were dead. Where is Tom? They have captured him?'

'No, he got away.'

Quickly I told him how Tom had managed to escape.

'Ah!' he exclaimed. 'It is true what Tom says: his sister Mulumbe is a very special person.'

I shook my head. 'Not special enough to save our food. Peter, the marauders have got the sacks of mealie meal.'

'Not this one,' he said, as with a wide grin he showed me the second sack of drought-relief mealie meal.

'And they have not got the fish,' a voice said from behind a tree.

'Tom!'

My brother appeared carrying the dried fish.

'How did you manage that?'

As we embraced, Tom whispered, 'I managed it because of you. I will never forget, Mulumbe Mudenda, that you are the cleverest girl in the world.' Turning to Peter he spoke louder. 'Now come on before they find us. We must get this food to the village. I can't wait to see the faces of those at home when they see the good news we are bringing.'

'Yes,' nodded Peter. 'There is no better news than that which the stomach can hear.'

But our happiness was short-lived. When we returned to the village Grandmother had already died.

The terrible knot of grief that I had seen bind Mutinta's family together, when they thought she was lost, now tied

Tom and I to the little ones. 'She was our world,' we shouted, wailing and sobbing. 'But now she is gone. She was our water, now her drops have been drunk by the earth. She was the keeper of our stories, now silence is all that is left at our fireside.'

The little ones stared up at us, eyes huge with sorrow. Magoyela clung to me as though she was drowning. She was so thin I could count her ribs, each one like a twig of firewood. 'My sister,' she sobbed, 'we are lost, we are lost without her.' Although her tears were drenching me, I did not stop her crying. I did not stop myself from crying. As Grandmother once said, some days are meant for tears. But when, I wondered, would the days for laughter ever come back?

In our grief I caught sight of my father standing by his hut. He had just returned from the city. I watched him bend down and lift a beer bucket to his lips. He was as dead to us as the one for whom we grieved. More so. For there are none so truly dead as those who no longer care about life.

'Mulumbe,' Magoyela whispered that night when the others were asleep, 'will Father look after us now?'

'No,' I replied. 'He will not look after us.'

'Who will then?'

'Tom is the head of the family now.'

'But what happens when Tom goes to the mines?'

I swallowed hard. 'Then I will look after you.'

'And if you go away, Mulumbe?'

'Magoyela, I will *always* look after you.'

My sister nodded. 'Grandmother told me you would keep us safe. She kept asking for you at the end.'

'What did she say?'

'So many strange things. I could not understand her. But she would not rest until I promised to give you a message.'

'A message?' I asked, barely able to control my voice.

'She said: 'Now Hare will need new tricks to survive'.'

'Hare?'

'She said that you would know what she meant. She said that you must remember the riddle as well. The last one she gave you. The most important one of all.'

'I am a cloud,' I whispered, 'I can blow anywhere.'

'What does it mean?'

'I do not know, Magoyela.'

'Well, whatever it means, Grandmother said you must solve it with your own life.

Burying Grandmother almost broke me. High above us the sky was bruised with vultures; they too were now tasting famine. As we stood at the grave, their shadows passed through us like ghosts. Grandmother was wrapped in a cloth and then lain in the earth. Her body had shrunk to such a size that it seemed once again I was watching them bury little Namaanza. The children clung to me. Olinji stood so close that I could smell his breath. His red, swollen eye followed every movement I made. It was only when Tom pushed his way between us that he moved back.

Tom was growing into a man. But for how much longer would he be able to protect me from Olinji? Soon he would be going to the mines. And then what? Olinji would come for me when there was no one else around. Next time there would be no escape.

I was to lose my brother's protection sooner than I had thought. The food we had brought from the district centre had given us a little strength but it ran out. Tom and Peter had to go back to wait for another relief delivery. Everywhere I went now Olinji seemed to follow me. It was like living with a hyena as my shadow. Yet, I had to carry on. I was mother, father and grandmother to Magoyela and the little ones.

The days went on and still Olinji did not make his move. One evening I was sitting alone by the fire while the little ones slept in the hut. The circle of firelight, once so reassuring and cosy, had become a yawning abyss, like the open jaws of Crocodile. Who could fill the gaps left by those I had lost?

All at once a shadow flitted beyond the light of the flames. It hovered there for a while as though watching me. The shadow took human form as it entered the circle of light. 'How are you, my beautiful, young woman.'

It was Stepmother. Ever since I had defied her, I had been waiting for this moment of reckoning. I knew that she never forgot anything. When would she start her beating? Or would it be worse than that? Yet she did not seem angry. She was not carrying her stick. 'Mulumbe,' she smiled, 'how are you?' Though totally at her mercy I could not bring myself to reply to the false friendship in her voice. 'Mulumbe,' she continued, 'why do you make your brothers and sisters starve?'

'What?'

'Why do you let them go hungry when you know how to feed them?'

Her words struck me far harder than any stick. 'If I could feed them I would.'

'You *can* feed them, young woman.'

'How?'

'All you have to do is marry Olinji. Then *he* will feed them.'

I knew at once that this was the trap I would never escape from.

'Don't you want to feed them, Mulumbe?' she asked.

I nodded.

'Then marry him. If you become his wife the children will be part of *his* family. He has plenty of food to go round. So you see, there is a way. And as soon as you agree he will pay the *luselo* and I will buy some food for the children. Maybe even some meat. Don't you think it will be nice to see Magoyela eat some lovely meat?' Her face narrowed like the sting of a scorpion. 'It is up to you. Save them, or kill them. What will you do?' Her voice dropped to a whisper. 'But first you must tell him that there is no curse.'

'Curse?'

'Yes. Olinji is worried that the old woman left a charm on you that would curse him if he tried to marry you.' Stepmother faltered uncertainly. 'That is why he has waited. Everyone knows the old woman was a friend of the *Sikatonga*. So tell me. *Is* there a curse, Mulumbe?'

Here was the chance of escaping my fate. If I let them believe in the curse, I would never have to worry about marrying Olinji, and Stepmother would never dare to be cruel to me again.

But was it so simple? *I* might be free, yet who then

would feed the children? Tom said he was going to send money from the mines, but when would he begin work, let alone get his first wage? Money was never paid promptly. Then there was the mine itself. That deep, dark stomach might swallow him as it had swallowed many others. Besides, older men were always buying young girls to be their wives. Why did I think I was any different? If I had to marry Olinji to save the little ones, then did I really have a choice? 'Mother,' I whispered, 'Grandmother was a good woman. There is no curse.'

Instantly Stepmother's fear became mocking laughter. I could still hear her cruel cackling as she slinked back into the darkness towards Olinji's hut.

I did not have to wait long before I heard him approaching. Out of breath, he was running. I looked into the hut. I could just make out the shapes of the sleeping little ones. Everything I did was for them.

But it wasn't Olinji coming for me. '*Kwasiya*, Mulumbe!'

'*Iyii*, Peter!'

'We must talk,' Peter said.

'I thought you were at the district centre.'

'I was. I have come from Tom. He says goodbye.'

'Goodbye?'

'Yes. And I am going with him. So I too must say goodbye.'

I sighed sadly. But, after all, maybe it was better that they both went before they knew what was going to happen to me. Then, at least, they would not have to carry the weight of my sad fate down with them into the mines. 'So, Peter, it is time for you to go to the mines then.'

'We are going further than that.'

'Further?'

'Mulumbe, we are going to the City of Gold.'

'The City of Gold?' A scorpion seemed to have stung me. The City of Gold was far, far away in a distant, cruel country. It was said that its streets were paved with gold, but they might as well be paved with crocodiles. Few who ever walked on them came back again. It was a human jungle where people thought nothing of killing for a calabash of beer. 'No,' I said quickly, 'you cannot go to the City of Gold.'

'We must.'

My voice rose in anguish. 'If you go there I will never see either of you again.'

'Mulumbe, Tom has done something terrible!'

A noise in the darkness made Peter swing round. But it was nothing, just one of the small innocuous creatures of the night. A pangolin going about his business.

He spoke quickly. 'Listen, Mulumbe, I cannot stay here long. We have been tracking the night marauders.'

'The night marauders?'

'They were at the district centre commandeering the drought relief. Tom waited for the one with the gun to be alone. The one that . . .' He paused. The shadows cast by the flames writhed over his face. 'You know, Mulumbe, he was the one who took your mother and hurt my sister. Tom waited until he could get him alone and then –'

I gasped in horror. 'He has killed him?'

'He struck him on the head with a stone. I do not know if he is dead. But now the marauders are looking for Tom. He is not safe here. He is not safe anywhere. That is why he must go to the City of Gold.' Peter began to edge away. 'Tom is waiting for me.'

I stared at him in disbelief. 'Will I ever see my brother again? Peter, will I ever see *you* again?'

'I will often see you, Mulumbe. Whenever I close my eyes. But I don't know when we will meet again. I must go now. Mulumbe, as soon as we get to the City of Gold we will find work. Then Tom will send you money. Do not think he will ever forget you. Do not think I will. Mulumbe, here is some food. It is mealie meal and fish.' He dragged a bag out of the darkness.

Looking at me, Peter's face was caught by one last tortured shadow of firelight, then he was gone. I watched him wading into the darkness, as though into the lake. His body showed its shape for a few more moments, then it was submerged in the great depths of night.

Day after day the sun-man poured his molten heat down on us from a cloudless sky. The grass and forest were seared white as the *Sikatonga*'s hair. It was the dry white season. Many moons would pass before the rains came back – if they did – and we could plant once more. Would I ever see the two boys again? I felt numb inside. But could not give up. Others were depending on me. I had become like mother Weaverbird. Would *my* nest also prove too flimsy? Olinji was our only hope for life.

I was to marry him at the next full moon. Soon we would receive the *luselo*. Until then, I had to find a way to feed the others. But when the food Peter gave us ran out and we still had not received a cent of the bride price, I was left with no other choice: 'Magoyela,' I said, waking her before dawn one morning, 'get the little ones ready. Today we are going to the fishing camp.'

'The fishing camp?'

'Yes. Our fishing camp on the lake.'

She clapped her hands together in delight. 'Oh,

Mulumbe, Grandmother was right: you *will* look after us. You are so clever to have got a fishing licence.'

I did not mention the fact that I had no licence and that if I was caught I would be sent to prison. What was the point in worrying her?

When we arrived at our old fishing camp on the lake even more trees were showing in the shallows. It was as though the drought was lifting back the blanket of the water to reveal the bones of the bodies sleeping under its surface. Now I could clearly see the forest Grandmother had talked about, the place she had walked through as a girl. The sight of it made me feel even lonelier.

It did not take long to find the old nets. We had stayed at the fishing camp so many times in the days when my father was still alive for us. How I had loved to watch him as his nets bulged with nourishing fish. Tom and Peter had returned here recently. I could see the charred ground where their fire had burnt.

Although the roof of the lakeside hut had fallen in and the dugout canoe had been holed, just to see the old camp again brought back so many happy memories. In the time since we had last been here as a family, vegetation had sprung up everywhere. When I went down to the boulders that used to be on the water's edge I thought I saw my father sitting patiently, mending his nets as I had seen him do so many times. But it was only a bush growing there. The bush did not smile and raise a hand to beckon me over as my father so often used to, but never would again.

With the little ones scanning the water for crocodiles and hippos, Magoyela and I fished. Many patrols had been reported: government rangers looking to catch the desperate people fishing illegally. But although we were there for some days, we saw no one. Many years ago Father had chosen our fishing camp because it was on a quiet inlet of the lake. Although he did not know it, his wisdom had saved his daughter from great danger.

When we had caught enough fish to last until the next moon, we returned to the village; Stepmother was furious. 'Where have you been, you bone in the throat?' Now that I had agreed to marry Olinji there was no need for her to be polite any more.

I told her about the fishing camp.

'Looking after yourself again,' she hissed. 'Filling yourself with fish while we go hungry.'

'My Mother,' I said, 'unless I find food for the children who else will feed them until we get Olinji's *luselo*? Has he not paid it yet?'

There was something so cruel in her eyes that I flinched as though from a snake. 'What do you mean *luselo*? What has the *luselo* got to do with those brats?'

'You said that we would use the *luselo* to feed the children.'

'Did you really think that I would waste a single cent on feeding that litter of rats? It has already been spent.'

'But the children –' I choked.

'It's time you forgot about those maggots. I don't think Olinji will be too pleased to have them squirming in his meat.'

'But you said he would look after them once we were married.'

'The world is full of hungry children. And before long you will have your own to feed.'

Trying to escape her laughter echoing in my ears, I found myself approaching my father's hut. There was nowhere else for me to go. I did not know what I was going to say. We had not spoken since the night my mother disappeared.

Although the dawn had passed and the morning was growing warm, my father had just got up. He sat hunched on his stool. 'Father,' I said quietly. Just as I had used to. But he did not answer. 'Father, it is Mulumbe.' He continued to stare ahead of himself, his one good eye narrowing as though trying to focus on something. Taking a deep breath I walked into the line of his sight. 'Father, your daughter is in trouble.' But even now he showed no sign of recognising my presence. I had been a fool to think he ever would.

Turning away from my silent father, I went into the forest. I did not know where I was going. I did not care. All I hoped was that I could lose myself and never be found. But I *was* found. By the last person I could have expected.

'Is that really you, Peter?'

'What are you doing in the forest, Mulumbe?'

'What are *you* doing?'

'I am coming home.'

'I thought you were going to the City of Gold.'

Peter's face was puffed up, his forehead gashed. 'What has happened to you? Where is Tom?' Averting his eyes in shame, Peter did not reply. 'Has he been hurt?'

'No, no, Mulumbe, your brother was all right . . . when I left him.'

'What is going on, Peter?'

'Mulumbe, meet me tonight on the path to the *Sikatonga*'s hut. I have an important message for you. I do not want anyone else to hear. What I have to say is for your ears only.'

That night, as soon as the little ones were asleep I set off along the path to the *Sikatonga*'s hut. An owl called. A thousand hidden eyes seemed to watch me from the forest.

'Have you been followed?' Peter asked, suddenly stepping out from behind a tree.

'I don't think so.'

'Let's make sure.'

We stood there in the darkness, listening. But there were only the endless songs of the night frogs. 'I'm sorry, Mulumbe, I did not mean to frighten you by bringing you here. But I had to know we would be alone.'

'Tell me about my brother.'

Peter sighed. 'We got as far as the border.'

'Together?'

He nodded. 'Then our real troubles began. You see, you need a passport. It's a little book. Without one they will not let you leave the country. As well as that you need what they call a visa. And money to bribe the officials. We had none of these things so instead we tried to walk along the high wire border fence until we found a place to cross. Many came with us. You would not believe how many people want to leave our country. We walked and walked but the sun set and still we had not found a place to cross. Mulumbe, there was a tragedy. In the night, one of the others was taken by a lion.'

'Ah!'

'But perhaps what happened when we returned to the border crossing was just as bad.'

The stars flickered and the moon-woman rose higher in the sky above us. It would not be long before she grew fat, and I became Olinji's bride. 'Mulumbe,' Peter began when he could speak again, 'we returned to the border crossing and waited. We had almost given up hope of finding a way through when God sent us help. At least I hope it was God.'

'What happened?'

'We met a man who helps people cross the border. They say that he is a priest. They call him Siana Sulwe.'

'The Hare,' I whispered for that is what those words mean in our language.

'Yes, and without him Tom would never have been able to cross.'

'Tom crossed the border?'

'He did. But I will not tell you how. It is too terrible to think of. Mulumbe, I was too frightened to do it. I tried to follow him in another way by clinging to the axle of a lorry. But I could not hold on long enough. I was lucky. When the border guards caught me, they –' He lifted a hand to the cuts and bruises on his face. 'These scars will heal. But what Tom had to do will give me nightmares for the rest of my life.'

The pain in his eyes made Peter seem no older than my little brother, Simonje. 'What did he have to do, Peter?'

'Please do not even ask me to speak of it, Mulumbe. I could never have done such a thing. And now, I am too ashamed to look you in the eye.'

'Ashamed?'

Peter shuddered. 'I was not man enough. Now, let me give you Tom's message: I am going, he said, but I *will* return. There will come a time when the government changes and the marauders are punished. On that day, and it might be soon, I will come back. Those were his words for you, Mulumbe. Until then he is going to send money home; enough for all of us . . . Are you crying? What is the matter? Is this not good news? Remember, you are not alone. I am here to help too.'

My voice fluttered like the nestlings of the weaverbird. 'It is too late.'

'Too late?'

'Yes. The good news has come too late. I am to be married.'

'What?' Peter's voice rang out so loudly in the night that it disturbed the owl into shrieking.

After the owl had quietened I told him about Olinji. 'So you see,' I said when I had finished, 'I also am too ashamed to look you in the eye.'

'No, Mulumbe, what you have done is no shame. What else could you do?'

'I have broken my promise.'

'What promise?'

'I swore to Namaanza and Kapu that I would look after our brothers and sisters. Now, even my promises are worthless. You see, they lied to me. Stepmother said Olinji would look after them. But now I know he never will. And without me who will care for them? They will be left to dry under the sun . . .'

Yet even as I spoke hope began to fly inside me. Its wings grew so powerful that it felt as though I was going to lift up from the ground. All was not lost! There *was* something that I could do to keep my promise. And to save myself. In fact, the *only* way to feed my brothers and sisters would also save me from my fate with Olinji.

'Peter,' My voice rang out clear as the stars above, 'I must cross that border myself.'

'What?'

'I am going to the City of Gold.'

'This is not like you, Mulumbe, to joke at a time like this.'

'I am not joking.'

'Then I do not understand what you are talking

about. Are you mocking me because of my fear? Is that what you mean?'

'No. No. No. I would never do that.' Throwing my head back, I spun round so that the moon-woman swirled. 'I mean that I am going to the City of Gold. *Really* going.'

Peter shook his head vigorously. 'Have you never heard the stories about the City of Gold? The people there hold out one hand to help you; with the other they knife you in the back. A man struggles to live in the City of Gold. What could a girl do? It is impossible. You might as well go to the lake and throw yourself in!'

'If I stay here I might as well do that too. When the moon plumps I must go to Olinji's hut. How long will the children survive without me to feed them?'

'But the money Tom sends –'

'I will be married by then. Do you think Olinji and Stepmother would ever let me spend money on the little ones? No, Peter, this is the only way. I must go to the City of Gold myself. When Tom writes I will know his address, then I will go and find him. Now I *know* he will make it. I feel it in my heart. We will work together in the City of Gold. We will –'

'Mulumbe, all of this, it is impossible.'

'No, Peter, with your help it *can* be done.'

'My help?'

'Oh Peter, I can do nothing without you. Only you can help me raise the funds for the journey. Only you can look after the little ones. Only you can be trusted to spend the money we send home.' My excitement was growing. 'They call it the City of Gold, don't they? Surely it won't be long before we've earnt enough for us both to come back. Maybe we will even have enough to build our own huts. By the lake. Oh Peter, I would love to live by the lake. And if we do really well then we could buy fishing licences. Peter, don't you see, we would never be hungry again. *And* we would not need Stepmother or Olinji. We could pay off the *luselo* and be free, free, free!' Grabbing Peter I spun him round and round.

'Mulumbe, you don't even know where Tom is yet.'

'He will write with his address.'

Faster and faster we danced until even Peter threw his head back and shouted: 'What is not possible for others, Hare Mulumbe can do.'

'And will you help me?'

'Will Honeyguide help Honeybadger? Yes, I will help you.'

That night I dreamt that I stood on the shore of the lake gazing at the outstretched arms of drowned trees.

Fishing Eagle's cry rang across the water. Then the lake narrowed to a river. And no longer was it the cry of the Fishing Eagle that I could hear but the voice of Grandmother. She was calling from the far bank. I smiled in my sleep. The old one had not forgotten me.

Peter and I began the next day. We decided not to tell Magoyela. She would try and dissuade me, or even follow me. When I had gone it would be Peter's job to explain. Surely they would forgive me when they understood that this was the only way I could look after them.

To raise the money Peter and I had to risk everything. We fished for many days, selling some of what we caught at the market. But there were more and more government boat-patrols. When they spotted us we would run into the bush as their bullets shredded the foliage. We collected worms, taking them to the tourist camps to sell as fishing bait to the government officials who sometimes stayed there. Often they slapped us and took what we offered, but occasionally they gave us a few dollars.

I had already learnt a little English from Tom and as we fished Peter taught me more. 'You will need it on your journey,' he said. 'Without it you will be blind.'

This new language amazed me. 'Ah,' I said. 'These words are so small. How can a sprig of *kampinumpinu* shrink to just: *grass*? And they are so quick too. My mouth will never be able to catch them. Listen to the word *wood*, it does not dance on my lips like *bubalubalu*. And how can the *chibulubulu* bird sing when it becomes: *dove*?'

As my vocabulary grew so did our money. We hid the cash in the hole of a tree, just like Baboon in the story of Hare's bus trip. But time was already running out. The moon was waxing a little every night and I still had not heard from Tom. Every time we took fish to the district centre we went to the post office. But there was never a letter with my name on.

'We have enough money now,' Peter said solemnly one day as we stood at the cash tree. 'But we still do not have his address.'

'Letter or not I must go before the new moon.'

'How will you find him?'

'I do not know how, all I know is that I *will*.'

My last night at home came. The next evening would bring the full moon. As I sat for the final time with my brothers and sisters round the fire I told them only the funniest of Grandmother's stories, imitating the animals as she had done, but inside my heart was like the weaverbirds' nest after Elephant's visit. How would I be able to find my brother in the vast jungle they call the City of Gold? Yet if I did not go, staying here instead to marry

Olinji, then life would dry from these little ones as quickly as it had from the weaverbird nestlings.

When the children fell asleep at last, I laid a finger on each of their foreheads. That single, light touch broke my heart. Early in the morning, well before dawn, I would be leaving. And they would wake to find me gone. 'Mulumbe?' Magoyela murmured in her sleep.

'Shh,' I whispered. 'Shh.'

As I soothed her, anger rose in me. Why did I have to go like this, turning my back on those I loved? Where was the justice in this world? But the anger did not last for long. I did not want anything to ruin my last memory of the little ones.

Peter was crouching by the fire when I emerged from the hut. I had not heard him come. 'Mulumbe, Olinji is coming for you tonight.'

'Tonight? But the moon is not full until tomorrow night.'

'I overhead him talking. He will wait no longer. You must go *now*.'

'Now?'

'This minute. Are you ready?'

'Oh Peter, am I really doing the right thing?'

'Mulumbe I was not going to tell you this but –'

'Tell me what?'

'A few days ago, just before your father disappeared again, he argued with Olinji. He said that you would not be his bride.'

'What?'

'He said he refused his permission.'

My mind whirled. Could it really be possible? Had my father come back to life at last?

'Do not get your hopes up, Mulumbe, Olinji gave him a bribe. Your father accepted it. That is why he has gone to the city. He has taken his money there. I am only telling you this now so that you know there is no other choice. You must go.'

So, my father had sold me off, like a goat.

'Come now, Mulumbe. I will go with you as far the bus stop. At least at the start of your journey, you will not be alone. Come on. Olinji might be here at any moment.'

The breaking dawn found us on a dirt road. 'Mulumbe, take this bag. Inside there is money and a blanket. The City of Gold is cold.'

'Peter, I know you will make the children understand why I had to go.'

'Of course I will Mulumbe, but –'

'What is it?'

'When you come home,' he began, his gentle voice

murmuring on the air like a butterfly feeling the rising warmth with its wings, 'may I hope to be the one who builds your hut by the lake? I would not hurt you. I would love you.'

The tenderness in his voice touched me to the core. For a moment we looked at each other without speaking. 'We must always hope, Peter.'

When he began talking again I could tell that he was forcing his voice to sound full of hope. '*You* can do it, Mulumbe. You can get to the City of Gold. You can become like the Hare. Where others fail, somehow *he* succeeds. Now, do you remember everything I have told you?'

'Yes, I am taking a bus just like Hare in the story.'

'It will only take you as far as the city. Although this is not the City of Gold, you must still be very careful.'

'And I mustn't sleep at the bus station.'

'It's too dangerous there. Follow the passengers away from the tall buildings and stone streets. Most of them will be going to the township. That is where the people live. Your brother and I passed the night there. Find a place to hide like we did. But make it a good spot. Mulumbe, at night a city is like the forest. It is dangerous to be there alone. Do not become a predator's victim.'

'Peter, what happens if I meet my father there?'

He shook his head. 'The city is full of people. Who is able to find one drop of water in a whole lake?'

'Then how will I ever find Tom?'

'Nothing is impossible for Hare. Remember our plan. The next day at dawn leave the township and go back to the bus station. Catch a bus to the border. At the border you will have to –' He broke off.

'Peter, what was it that you could not do?'

'Why bring down bad luck on the day when you need only good? At the border you must look for the man they call Siana Sulwe. Without him there is no way across. I think he might know where Tom has gone.'

'I will recognise him by his large beard and laugh.'

'Yes, he has the biggest laugh you will ever hear. When you hear it you know that you have found the one individual in a thousand that you can trust. Good luck, Mulumbe. It is a long journey and now I must leave you. If you remember anything I say then it is this: do not walk through the City of Gold at night. Do you promise me not to walk through the City of Gold at night?'

'I promise.'

And with that he was gone.

PART TWO: . . . *I CAN BLOW ANYWHERE*

INTO THE UNKNOWN

On either side of the road the same ancient termite mounds rose like a giant's jagged teeth, the same hornbills bickered in the same trees, and the same red earth lay sweet with dew beneath my feet; but already I felt that I had strayed into a different world.

I had not been waiting long when somebody slipped out of the bush. A very tall woman about the age my mother would have been. Sitting down on the roadside, she stared at me. I looked up and then down the long length of the red road. Although it seemed to stretch forever, there were no vehicles in sight. When I glanced back at the woman, she was still gazing at me.

Could she sense that I carried money? I clutched my bag a little closer and carefully peeked inside. Peter had also given me some *nsima* wrapped in a strong leaf for freshness. And a dress. It was Mutinta's. Even in her sorrow, she had not forgotten me. I fingered the material, remembering the day she got it from the missionary priests. It was before the night marauders had seized her. My eyes misted so that I almost did not see the last thing in the bag. Peter had given me one of Fishing Eagle's feathers. Perhaps one day I might stand with him by the lake and watch Eagle fly again. One day . . .

'What are you doing, girl?'

The tall woman's sudden words jolted me. 'I am catching the bus,' I replied, stuffing the dress and feather back inside the bag.

'I have never seen you before.'

I shaded my face with a hand. Olinji had some relatives close to here. The last thing I should do was leave a trail that could be followed.

'Where are you going?' she asked, adding when I did not reply, 'Where have you come from?'

'Mother,' I replied respectfully, 'I am just making a journey.'

'You don't know where you have come from and you don't know where you are going. That will be some journey!'

As she continued to study me in silence the heat haze coiled itself over the road like a silver snake. Gradually the haze began to promise something more solid. Slowly an object took shape. Above it hung a cloud of dust, like that raised by the hooves of a huge herd of buffalo. I remembered the same thick cloud of dust hanging above the drought-relief lorry. The bus was coming.

So this was what Hare and Baboon travelled in. The top of it – where Baboon had been thrown in his sack – was piled high with luggage. The vehicle seemed to lean heavily to one side. When the sound of the labouring engine reached us I thought again of the buffalo herd, the strong beasts coughing and bellowing to the rising sun. Then we heard their hooves: the thunderous rattling of loose metal. I ducked into the bush and changed from my torn T-shirt and old skirt into Mutinta's lovely dress. Now no one would think that I was just a stupid bush girl who could be easily tricked.

When I came out from behind the trees the bus had arrived. A terrible stench rose in thick clouds from a pipe at its back, like the steam lifting from fresh dung.

'You getting on, girl?' A voice demanded. 'Or just admiring Tuff Boy?'

The driver was leaning over his wheel staring at me.

Without knowing who Tuff Boy was and half-choking with fumes, I nodded. But before I could mount the steps to the bus somebody reached out from behind and grabbed at my bag. I clung on as hard as I could.

'What's the matter with you?' the man who was

trying to get my bag demanded. He was wearing a black peaked hat.

'She thinks you are stealing it, man,' the driver laughed.

'Stealing it?' The man let go of the bag and lifting his hat scratched his bald head. 'But I take everyone's luggage. I'm the *Windi*. Haven't you ever heard of a *Windi*?' Having thrown up the tall woman's bags on top of the bus, he scrambled up a ladder fixed to the back of the vehicle and tied the luggage securely.

'Oh, I remember,' I said. 'Like the story of Hare and Baboon.'

'*Yebo!*' laughed the driver. 'And *he's* the baboon. So come on, girl, throw up your bag. Tuff Boy's got a timetable to keep, you know.'

But still I did not let go.

'I don't think she's going to give it up, man,' the *Windi* laughed. 'What you got in there that's so precious, girl?'

'Let her take it inside,' said the driver. 'It's small enough to fit on her knee.'

The *Windi* shrugged then gave an ear-splitting whistle. The engine throbbed into life. Gingerly I climbed up on to the bus. The vibrations beat like a thousand hearts beneath my feet.

'Hey, girl,' chuckled the driver. 'You ever been on a bus before?' He shot the vehicle forward. I only just managed to keep on my feet. Through the open door, I could see the road moving. My stomach bubbled like a pot of *nsima*. The bus stopped again. I was thrown forward. The driver guffawed. 'Now, where you want to go, girl?'

'Please, Sir, I am going to the city.' Carefully I handed over the correct money as Peter had instructed.

The bus was packed. As well as the people there were bags of mealie meal, wooden cages with hens and baskets full of produce. These were the lucky ones, the ones who, like Olinji, were not starving. They had goods to sell in the city where prices were high. The passengers gossiped and laughed, a sound I had forgotten. A baby on a mother's back giggled at me. With an ache I pictured Kapu and Namaanza, and Magoyela's arms thin as Anteater's tongue.

The engine roared, the bus rattled, and a choking cloud of smoke drifted over the passengers. Hugging my bag and coughing, I could not get my balance. Tuff Boy lurched down the road. I staggered down the aisle. There was nowhere to sit. 'What are you doing?' People demanded irritably. 'Watch where you're going, you stupid girl!' Losing my footing, I fell flat on my face.

Gently someone raised me to my feet. It was the woman who had waited with me. 'Do not worry, you will soon get used to it.' She made room for me at the window beside her.

The forest flashed by like a dream. Every now and again a startled hornbill crashed from an overhanging branch. From time to time a panic-stricken buck would spring right out in front of us. I gripped the seat. Riding a bus was like riding the back of a stampede.

Yet despite the peculiar sense of movement, and the stench of fumes, every moment I sat here shortened the distance separating me from Tom.

Large potholes caused Tuff Boy to jump like a jackal hunting rats in the long grass. When we began to climb into the hills, his engine laboured so that the herd of buffalo became a creeping, vibrating tortoise.

How many times had I stared at these hills from our village and never once had I dreamt that I too would climb them! Tom had wandered here many times, grazing the goats, and now here I was following him. The higher we rose, the greater was the view until I could see the whole of the lake spread out over the valley. It was as though I was seeing it for the first time. I had never realised that it was so big. The span of its silvery wings mesmerised me like the wings of a giant eagle spread in flight.

At each stop people got on, somehow squeezing their

way into the already crowded seats. Up and down his ladder the *Windi* climbed. When he had tied all the bags, he whistled piercingly and the driver gave a shout as though of encouragement and Tuff Boy sprang forward.

The road continued to fly higher and higher, and the ground at our side fell away to a deep ravine. At the bottom of the ravine, lying there like the carcass of a giant elephant, was the wreck of another bus. We mounted a particularly steep rise and when we came down on the other side, the lake had gone from sight. We had crossed the hills. We were descending to a different landscape. From now on everything would be strange.

A loud crack rang out. I ducked with the instinct of those who have had a gun fired at them. As though shot, Tuff Boy seemed to stumble. He broke from the driver's control then began to skid towards the edge of a sheer drop.

People screamed. Hens flapped furiously. Luggage and baskets vomited down the aisle. Then something struck me on the side of the head and I tumbled into my own ravine of darkness.

When I came round the bus had come to a halt. There was a chaos of coughing, moaning and crying. Dust choked the eyes. I felt a hand in mine. It was the tall woman. 'Come quickly,' she said.

'Where are we going?'

Dazed, I allowed myself to be led down the aisle. 'Hurry up, girl,' she urged. 'Broken-down vehicles have a tendency to blow up!'

But Tuff Boy did not blow up. He had slid right to the edge of a precipice. Another few feet and he would have plunged down. The woman climbed up to the top of the bus and carefully retrieved her luggage. I still carried mine. Even when I had been knocked unconscious I had not let go.

'We are lucky to be alive,' she said, sitting beneath a tree.

I nodded my throbbing head. The rest of the passengers were emerging – groggy and disorientated as termites fumigated by the smoke of the *bubalubalu* wood. I could not believe that no one had been badly hurt. It was amazing how quickly everyone seemed to be recovering.

'We're used to it,' the woman said. 'It happens a lot. Are you all right?' She laid her arm tenderly round my shoulder. For that instant it was as though my mother had come back. 'Close your eyes,' she whispered, 'you have had a nasty shock.'

When I opened my eyes the dizziness had cleared, although I still felt the throbbing. But what I saw made me forget any discomfort. The woman had brought out two hardboiled hen's eggs. 'So you are going to the city?' she said.

'Yes,' I replied, my eyes swimming at the sight of food.

'What has happened to you, girl?'

'Nothing has happened,' I just managed to reply.

'I don't believe you. Only something very bad would force a young girl like you to travel to the city on her own. It is a very bad place.'

From somewhere in the forest beyond the road, hornbills bickered. I tried to concentrate on the familiar sound but the food so near to me was like a punch in the stomach. It was such a long time since I had eaten anything other than *nsima* or dried fish. The woman peeled the eggs then laid one on my lap.

'Why?' I asked.

'Eat,' she replied.

Now I understood what she was up to. She knew I was hungry. And that I had money. When I had eaten the food she would charge me highly for it. Olinji had done this kind of thing before. With a trembling hand I reached into my bag. The roll of notes that Peter and I had so painstakingly assembled seemed to pulse in my hand like the neck of a hen. I did not care if she was going to cheat me. At that moment I would have parted with every single cent just for one egg.

'Put your money away, girl,' the woman said quickly.

'But –'

'Eat,' she soothed. 'It's a gift.'

I clapped my hands together by way of thanks. I wanted to shovel the whole lot into my mouth, but forced myself to eat slowly, savouring each tiny piece.

'It is a long, long way to the city,' the woman said when I had finished.

Despite Peter's many warnings, I decided to trust the woman. 'I am not just going to the city. I am going across the border to the City of Gold.'

'The City of Gold!' I saw the shock register on her face. 'Did he beat you?'

'Who?'

'Your father, or your brother? Or your husband? The person you are running from.'

I shook my head. 'I am not running from anyone. I am running *to* someone.'

'Well, child, you know your own business. You don't need me to tell you how hard it is for a man to reach the City of Gold. Let alone a young girl like you. Crossing the border will be hard enough. And then when you get there . . .' She reached out and her hand rested on my brow for a moment like a butterfly resting on a flower.

Then she opened one of her bags and brought out a pair of boy's shorts, a T-shirt and a cap. 'These are my son's, but your need is greater. Put them on. Where you are going it is better to be a boy. I know you are just a girl, but you will be a woman in many men's eyes. And that could . . . complicate things.'

I looked at her closely. Something told me she was right. 'You can have my dress as an exchange,' I said.

'No, my child. Keep the dress. You will not always have to be a boy. And a word of advice: if you are going to the city it is better that nobody sees what you have in your bag. The sight of money is like scattering meat for vultures.'

I went behind a tree and changed. When I came out I had left Mulumbe Mudenda behind.

'What will you call yourself?' the woman asked.

'What is your son called?'

'My son is called Banyu.'

'Then I am Banyu. Thank you for all your help.'

'You were right to trust me, but where you are going there are very few who you should trust. You must trust no one, but to get there at all you will have to trust *someone* –'

'Ah,' I said. 'That sounds like a riddle.'

'It is the riddle of life.'

We rested through the heat of the day under the tree while the driver and the *Windi* fiddled with the engine of the bus. At last, miraculously, it burst into life. Quickly we all remounted. Then, with a piercing whistle from the *Windi* and a shout from the driver, Tuff Boy lurched on his way again.

The kind woman was not going all the way to the city. When she had got off the bus, she stood at the side of the road waving until we could no longer see each other. A man sat in her place. His greedy elbows pushed me right up against the rattling window. I was glad that I had left Mulumbe behind that tree. But I sensed that even Banyu was going to have great difficulty in reaching the City of Gold.

The red road seemed to be stretching ahead forever when suddenly the surface below our wheels became smoother. The windows did not rattle so crazily. The engine no longer laboured quite so much. We were on a tar road. Faster and faster we drove, until the bush outside became a bewildering blur. Tuff Boy's stampeding hooves had become the graceful lope of the giraffe.

Turning on to an even bigger road, all at once I saw more traffic than I had ever thought there to be in the whole world. The speed of these vehicles was dizzying.

Alongside them we were like a pangolin bumbling through the bush.

A huge lorry throbbed by, only inches from Tuff Boy's metal ribs. I gasped. As though from nowhere a car burst past. The back end of another bus scraping against the road showered us with sparks. Reaching into my bag I fingered the feather. It was the only way I could remain as calm as the rest of the passengers and not draw attention to myself. Everything in this new world seemed too fast and sharp for the soft body I had been born with. The feather seemed the only tenderness left.

The hours passed and evening fell. But the darkness brought a new terror. The cars and lorries sprouted bright, dazzling eyes that seemed to scour the night searching for me. I pulled the cap over my face and huddled into my seat, but they still found me. Even when I closed my eyes I could feel the scalding probe of these headlights. Then all at once the night itself seemed to catch fire.

The flames cast a scalding white light that grew and grew until the whole world seemed to be blazing. I forced myself to look. In the blanching light, shapes were rising. The shapes were buildings. More buildings than I could ever have imagined. I looked around at the other passengers. They were quietly gathering their luggage.

The bus stopped. The people got off. I watched them walking into the flaming night.

'Hey you,' the driver called. 'Time to say night-night to Tuff Boy.' I hugged my bag tighter. 'He isn't a hotel. What's the matter; never been to the city before?'

'Sir, everything is so bright.'

His laugh was deep. 'It's electricity, bush boy. They call it electricity.'

FOUR WHEELS

Like a fish carried far from the lake in Eagle's talons and dropped in the middle of dry land, I stepped off the bus.

Was it night or day here? The moon was in the sky but the shadow following me was carved sharply on the hard concrete ground as though by an afternoon sun. Buildings rose above me like giant termite mounds, each one tall enough to harbour a thousand black mambas. I did not dare look up. People were everywhere, their voices humming. It was like being in a great nest of bees. But all I saw were feet. More feet than I had ever seen before. And most of them were enclosed in shoes! Each pair was different. Could there really be so many different types of shoes? The pavement drummed to their rhythm. Maybe these feet would lead me to the township.

When the night became much darker and the concrete gave way to rough ground, I finally looked up. The tall buildings had gone. There before me was a vast open space littered with huge heaps of rubble and flickering

161

with countless oil-drum fires. Around each of these makeshift fires, silhouetted figures were gathered. Close to me a baby started crying. I heard a woman hush the infant. Then I picked out the shape of a mother gently rocking her child. Was this the township? Here were the people but where were their homes? I walked on. A man shouted, then someone began to weep. Very, very far away someone screamed. It is incredible how far the sound of a scream can travel in the night.

Skirting the mounds of rubble, careful to keep in the shadows, I passed families eating, old women talking and a group of men squatting round a particularly large drum. The shape of the bucket they were sharing was all too familiar. So was the smell of its contents. Was my father one of these men drinking beer? Not waiting to find out, I hurried on.

Some way ahead I found the ground littered with what appeared to be logs. They lay across my path like waiting crocodiles. Carefully picking my way over them, I only found out what they actually were when one of them tripped me up.

Before I could get back up, the log had grown a face. Its eyes were staring into mine. Then it sprouted shoulders too, and a torso. The logs were sleeping bodies. But this one had woken up. Screaming in a language I did not understand, it reared at me. I scrambled away.

Scurrying up a mound, I clambered over bricks and broken window frames. It felt safer here. Taking out my blanket, I placed it on top of what must have been a door. A little car made from wire lay in the wreckage beside me: a child's toy.

I stretched out under my blanket. If only the earth would fold itself over me and protect me from prying eyes. All at once I understood the shyness of many of the forest creatures, the shyness that sends them running and scuttling at the sight of a human, a shyness in which no hole can be deep enough, no hollow properly secure. If I could have buried my way to the bottom of the heap of rubble, I would have done.

As I lay there waiting for the dawn, I stared at the sky above. No Grandmother lay close. No Tom, no Magoyela, no little ones. All I had was Peter's feather.

I pulled the blanket over my head and cowered like a rat in the rafters of a hut when a python comes through the door. Although I was shivering it was the cold of my loneliness that really pierced me.

My limbs had stiffened and I was chilled to the bone when suddenly the blanket was ripped away and a face leered down at me. There was the familiar stench of sour beer. Olinji had found me.

But it wasn't Olinji.

A different man was tottering above me, haranguing me in a language I could not understand. Just then a shockingly close voice whispered. I shrieked. It was as though a beetle had crawled into my ear. A second man was kneeling over me. He had crept up without my realising. He was holding a thick, crooked stick.

His head was huge; his features chewed and pinched like a pumpkin that has been gnawed by rats. Before I could get away he had hooked the crook of his stick round my arm. While the man above continued to rage, the pumpkin head hissed at me in the same incomprehensible language. 'I am sorry, Sir,' I said in the broken English Tom and Peter had taught me, 'I do not understand.'

'You speak English?' Pumpkin Head demanded. 'Well, you're in his place, man.'

'His place?' I replied.

He gestured at the rubble and the huge man raging above me. 'This is his home-sweet-home.'

'Home-sweet-home?' I managed to stammer.

'His house, man, his house. This is where he lived. Until last week. The government just knocked his residence down.'

'I'm sorry, Sir.'

'Well. I'll inform the president of your feelings.'

Pumpkin Head's sudden laugh was a terrible, hollowed-out echo, which died abruptly when he called up to his companion. 'He says he's sorry, man.' His companion snarled and shouted incomprehensibly. 'I don't think he likes you, man,' Pumpkin Head announced, then abruptly lost his temper. 'You damned squatter. Moving in on a man's property.'

He spoke with a lisping, whistling sibilance that sprayed my face. In his agitation, the hook of his stick fell slack on my arm. Seizing the opportunity, I jumped to my feet. The man above me lunged. Ducking just in time, I felt fingers brush against my cap. Before I could get away, Pumpkin Head swung his stick. I leapt over it then scampered down the mound but already the great round head was rolling after me. Reaching the bottom I ran past one of the oil drums, then another. The silhouetted figures warming themselves did not even look at me.

After a while I dared to look over my shoulder. It had been a narrow escape. But at what cost? I had left my bag behind on the mound. Without it my journey to the City of Gold would be impossible. As I stood there in despair wondering what to do, a peculiar squeaking set the hair on the back of my neck bristling like Porcupine when she senses danger. It grew louder. The next moment my legs were knocked away from underneath me. Crashing to the ground I found Pumpkin Head waiting for me. He was grinning. Still seemingly on his knees, he was brandishing the stick with which he had scythed me down.

'I'm sorry, Sir, I did not know your friend . . .'

'Who says he's my friend, man?' he demanded. 'Who says anyone's got a friend in a place like this?' Then, to my surprise, he switched into my language: 'Many people visit my hut, but I have no family. Who am I?'

'You are the city,' I said.

His eyes widened. 'You understood my riddle, boy?'

As I nodded I saw that he had my bag.

'You're from the lake?'

'Yes.'

His eyes sparkled. He no longer looked so terrifying. 'Well, well, well, a bush boy just like me. Just as well you met me, man. This place has gone crazy. Last week it was a township; today it's a disaster area. It's been bulldozed. Everywhere you go there are mad fellows. What's your name, boy?'

'Banyu,' I said, forming the strange name carefully on my lips.

'Well, Banyu. Everyone calls me Four Wheels.'

It was then that I saw why he still seemed to be kneeling. The man had no legs. His body was propped on a buggy, which he propelled by using his stick as an oar. A wave of horror and pity crashed over me.

'So what brings you here, Banyu?'

'Oh,' I said, thinking fast. 'I am meeting my brother.'

'Who's your brother?'

'I don't think that you will know him.'

'I know everyone. And they know me. Just ask anyone here for Four Wheels.' He stared at me then smiled. 'Come on, man, you can't sleep out here. I'll take you to a better place.'

The wheels of his buggy squeaked loudly as he moved off. I followed. How was I going to get the bag back?

'So what's in here, little brother Banyu?' He held it up.

'Nothing,' I said. If he looked inside he would find the money.

'You got money?' His wide nostrils flaring, he began to snuffle. His sunken eyes closed with concentration as he buried his nose in the bag. 'Four Wheels smells money.'

What would a boy do in a situation like this? Coiling my leg I kicked Four Wheels as hard as I could. Grunting, he toppled off his buggy. I grabbed my bag. 'No offence, man,' he called after me as I ran. 'I just wanted to bring it over for you. Where are you going? Hey, don't run away. Don't leave me.' Ignoring his pleas, I continued my escape. 'Help me, man. How can I get back on the trolley by myself?' The sudden desperation in his voice made me stop. I turned. He was still lying where I had knocked him. 'Give me a hand,' he pleaded. 'If you leave me like this, they'll eat me, man.'

'Eat you?'

He mimed a rat eating grain. 'Every little scrap of me.'

'Who will eat you?'

'The *tsotsis*. Don't tell me you've never heard of a *tsotsi*. You really have just come from the lake, haven't you? Come here and I'll explain.' I took a few steps back to where he lay. 'A *tsotsi* is a thief. A *tsotsi* would rob a sleeping baby. A *tsotsi* would eat your skin if he could. Hurry up, man, help me back on to the trolley. One might come along at anytime.'

When I got up close to him I could see that the hand he was holding out to me was huge; the fingers curled like the noose of a snare. Before he lost his legs he must have been very tall. Come on, man, I'm begging you. If a man has no legs, you've got to give him a hand.' The moment I reached out, he grabbed me. His grip tightened. Then he tugged and I was nearly pulled off my feet. Like a fish flipping from land to water, he managed to climb back up on to his buggy. 'I like you.' He grinned. 'I definitely like you. And that's why I'm going to help you. Come with me, bush boy. I know a hole where the *tsotsis* can't fit.'

Maybe it was hearing my language spoken in a strange place; maybe it was because the other options seemed worse; for some reason I decided to trust him.

I followed the squeaking trolley round great piles of rubble and many oil-drum fires but when I found myself back among tall buildings near the bus station I hung back. 'Don't stop, don't stop, man,' Four Wheels cried. 'The *tsotsis* feast here. *Yebo* they'll drink your eyes.'

He led me down the alleys that lay between the high buildings. We no longer passed anyone. Was he luring me to where a robbery would have no witness? Was he himself a ravenous *tsotsi*? At last he stopped. 'This is the place,' he said. 'You'll be safe here.'

It was totally dark. No moon, no street lamps.

'Don't worry, man,' Four Wheels whispered. 'You're going to be glad you came with me.'

'Why?' I asked.

'You'll see, bush boy. Oh *yebo*, you'll see.'

I quickly made my plan. The only one I could think of in this dark corner. I would stay awake until dawn then go back to the bus station and continue with my journey. All I had to do was to keep my wits about me and pretend to be Banyu: the boy who was meeting his brother, the boy who could kick like a zebra if crossed. Even when confronted by a deadly snake or spider, staying still is often the best form of defence.

I sat down. At least the ground was so cold that there would be no danger of me falling asleep.

I could only see the whites of my companion's eyes, and hear the rat-squeak of his trolley each time he shifted position on it. When he suddenly broke the silence his voice was surprisingly gentle. 'When did you last see the lake, man?'

'This morning,' I replied.

'This morning?' The whites of his eyes seemed to flash with longing. 'We're a long way from home, Banyu, and, believe me, it gets a little longer every day. I suppose you're wondering how I lost my legs? It's not a long story. In fact the legs were longer. One night I got so drunk that I couldn't stand. When I woke up they had been pulped like pumpkins. A lorry had run over me. You wouldn't believe it but I used to be tall.' His rueful laugh vibrated in the confined space. 'Perhaps if that hadn't happened I would have walked home by now. Just tell me one thing, Banyu, does Fishing Eagle's call still seem to fill the world?'

'Yes,' I replied. 'It does.'

'I would give anything to hear her again.'

Reaching into the bag I brought out the feather. 'Feel this,' I said.

I could feel his hand groping in the darkness. A single heavy finger stroked the softness. 'Banyu, boy,' he said, 'take care. There are worse things to lose here than your legs, man. I've been Four Wheels for so long that I can't even remember my real name.'

'Why did you come here?' I whispered.

'The soil in the villages around the lake is too thin. I grew sick of being hungry. Maybe that's why you're here too. I mean look at you. No offence, man, but I've seen more meat on a mealie stalk.' He squeaked with laughter again. 'I suppose you could say that I swapped my legs for a full stomach. Beware of such expensive transactions, man.'

But actually it was no longer cold in this hidden spot. In fact, it was growing warm. When I happened to touch the wall behind me, I realised why. The bricks radiated heat.

'Oh yes, man,' said Four Wheels scratching his back lovingly against the warming wall. 'Mother has lit the cooking fires.'

The night passed slowly. If only Grandmother were here to play riddles, but I knew that she would not have understood. For two people to share a riddle they must share a world. The city was a world she did not know: a story with unrecognisable characters. I pictured Tom and the little ones I had left behind. The night we had eaten the honey flickered before my eyes as though I were standing in the shadows watching the others from beyond the light of the fire.

At last, even here on this secret rat run, distant rumours of dawn began to reach me. A small stream of light flowed in. The sound of traffic intensified. And most strange of all, a rich aroma filled the air.

The smell stirred in me a distant memory. For a long time I could not work out what it was. Then I remembered. When I had gone with my father to the district centre he had bought me a doughnut. This delicious smell was baking bread. The warm building at my back was a bakery. I breathed in deeply.

Lulled by the warmth and the soothing aroma, I must have fallen asleep because I woke to a sour breath scouring my face. Four Wheels was bending right over me, rifling through the bag. 'I'm so hungry,' he whined. 'So, so hungry.'

'I have no food,' I replied, yanking the bag from him.

'No food?' In the light of the morning his pumpkin head looked as though it had been chewed even more in the night. 'But I'm hungry.' All at once an idea seemed to strike him. 'Hey, bush boy, want to know a secret?' He pointed up to a window in the high wall of the bakery. His voice dropped as though he was sharing the greatest secret of his life. 'Through that little glass mouth is more food than you could eat. I saw inside there once, man. There were huge loaves of bread everywhere. I mean, a whole room of bread. Enough to fill every belly in your village, and mine.' He sighed as though unable to believe his own memory. 'The number of times I've sat here and wished I was a bird so that I could fly right up. You see, they leave that little window open. If someone got up there, they could crawl through.' He rapped the stumps where his legs had been. 'I'd go there myself but they cut my wings off, man. Of course you'd have to be pretty thin to get in, it's not a large window –' Breaking off, his deep-set eyes sharpened. 'Hey, bush boy, I bet *you* could fit through it!'

I looked up. The smell of baking bread was intoxicating. It seemed that I wasn't only smelling it with my nose but with my ears too, as though it was whispering to me. Then, I realised that I had begun to chew, as though I was eating it already. I was drunk with the smell of fresh bread.

'Bush boy, why don't you just climb up through that little window and get us some of that bread?'

'But that's stealing.'

'Stealing?' Four Wheels shook his head indignantly. 'That's not stealing.'

'The police –'

'What do the police care about a loaf of bread when they're allowed to thieve anything they want from us? Lesson number one, bush boy: the only difference between an honest man and a thief is an empty stomach.' He looked at me narrowly. 'But didn't I tell you?'

'Tell me what?'

'The men in the bakery know me. They always leave a few loaves for Four Wheels.' His eyes worked quickly. 'You see it was a bakery lorry that ran over me. It's compensation, man. You'd be doing me a great favour if you'd just go up through that little window and collect those loaves for me.'

Without really realising what was happening I found myself being hoisted on to Four Wheels' shoulders. Taking my weight with only a slight grunt, he lifted up his arms like the drowned trees of the lake. '*Yebo*, you're thin enough to find a way through. Stand on my hands, man,' he whispered excitedly, hefting me up. 'Now, can you see that little hole in the bricks?'

'Yes.'

'Can you reach it?'

'It's a long way up.'

'Try!'

Lifting my leg as high as I could, I secured a foothold in a little cavity in the side of the wall.

'Now up you go, bush boy!'

The promise of baking bread helped me to spring from the cavity to where a protruding brick provided another foothold. 'Hee-hee,' giggled Four Wheels. 'Just like Honeybadger up that old honey tree.'

I found myself gripping the ledge of the small window. It *had* been left open. I pulled it wider, but it was still very narrow. I only just managed to squeeze myself through.

For a while the wonderful smell simply overpowered me. It was exactly as Four Wheels had said. On the far side of the large room were countless loaves of bread all stacked like bricks in a wall. 'Are you there?' Four Wheel's whisper rose up from below.

'Yes,' I replied looking down through the window.

'What are you waiting for then?'

'Which ones are yours?'

'What do you mean?'

'Where do they put the loaves they leave for you.'

'Oh that. Just take any.'

I crept as deftly as a civet cat but halfway across the wide room one of the floorboards creaked beneath my feet. I froze in horror. The noise seemed to echo loudly in the large room.

'Get a move on, bush boy, we can't hang about here all day,' urged Four Wheels.

Grabbing two loaves I carried them back across to the window.

'Just throw them down, bush boy.'

I did as he said.

'But where are its friends?'

'How many do they leave for you?'

'Take as many as you can carry. They owe me for a few weeks.'

This time, although I was doubly careful, the floorboard creaked again, as though the room was shouting its protests against my presence. I grabbed as many loaves as I could and threw them down. Four Wheels began to shove them in a sack. 'I'd better come down,' I said.

'No, no. Once the rat's in the granary does it leave after one bite?'

'But someone might have heard me.'

'I've told you, they're friends of mine.'

Hadn't he said that no one had friends in a place like this? But I was still too mesmerised by the smell of bread to argue so, heedless of the talkative floorboard,

I went back to get some more. In a fever I scooped up the loaves.

At that moment angry shouts erupted from below. 'Thief! Thief!'

'Four Wheels!' I cried, throwing the bread through the window.

But he was not there. The telltale squeak-squeak of his buggy was just fading from earshot. The shouts grew louder. He had tricked me. Panicking I squeezed myself through the window. It seemed much higher now than it had done when I was climbing up. And impossible to descend. I could not see the footholds.

A door in the far wall was flung open. Angry voices swarmed into the room. Footsteps thundered across the squeaking floorboards.

My journey was over. I would be thrown in prison for certain. Or worse. I had not even been able to reach the border, let alone the City of Gold. I had not learnt Hare's cunning. Instead I was the one who had been easily tricked. Unless . . . Taking a deep breath I dangled from the window ledge, then dropped.

AT THE BORDER

It was only when the bus finally pulled out of the city that I allowed myself to believe I really had escaped.

Dropping from the high window, I had remembered Hare rolling when he was thrown from Tortoise's shell. Hitting the ground, I did the same thing myself. In this way I avoided breaking bones. Snatching up the bag Four Wheels had left behind, I stuffed my loaves inside and scampered away. Reaching an open thoroughfare, I quickly melted into the crowd.

I managed to find the bus station. But the bus was not leaving until late in the afternoon. I hid there all day, pretending to belong to one queue after another, I stood with my head down and the cap pulled over my face. As the people came and went, I expected any moment to hear the police come charging in to seize me. I did not dare to eat the stolen bread or even go out to the pavement where some women were selling food from a cooking pot.

Once I thought I saw my father joining the queue

behind me but when I dared to look more closely it was not him. Just another drunkard whose eyes had grown too used to gazing at the bottom of a beer bucket to see any further.

But the police never came and so here I was in another bus on my way to the border. There I would have to find Siana Sulwe. A man with a large beard and an even bigger laugh. *When you hear it,* Peter had said, *you will know that you have found the one individual in a thousand who you can trust.* This man would get me across the border but only if I could do whatever had terrified Peter.

Through the bus window the tall buildings of the city were fast falling behind. How could anyone ever get used to this kind of travel? I reached into the bag. My fingers brushed tantalisingly against the fresh bread. What was it that Four Wheels had said? *The only difference between an honest person and a thief is a full stomach.* My stomach was empty. Closing my eyes, I tore off a hunk and opened my mouth.

When I opened my eyes I saw that the person sitting across the aisle from me was staring at my still chewing mouth. She was a girl about my age with red braids in her hair. Her eyes held a hunger that I recognised all too well. I ripped off another piece of bread and held it out. She shook her head. 'Go on,' I whispered, stretching across the aisle. At last, clapping her thanks and bearing the weight of the gift with two hands, she accepted.

Together we ate half of the loaf. Her smile of gratitude was like the dawn. But there was something sad about it too. Like the sun that rises on the day of a sorrowful anniversary.

Outside, evening was falling over a rural landscape. Through the window, huts dotted the horizon. It felt good to be away from the city. The girl and I smiled at each other. Although we had not spoken, we were friends. I pushed to one side of my mind the ordeal that lay ahead. Somehow I *would* find the courage that Peter lacked. The huts and trees continued to fly by outside. I was like a cloud drifting above them. I could blow anywhere . . .

'All off! All off!'

The rough voice of the driver thrust me from my dreams of drifting. Everyone else, including the girl with red braids had already disembarked.

I had slept all night. Stepping off the bus, the rising sun played gently on my face. But I could not enjoy its warming balm for long. All the other passengers were already walking up a hill.

'Is this the border, Sir?' I asked the driver uncertainly.

His hand swept a weary path up the lift of land. 'Go up there and you'll see.'

The first thing I saw when I reached the top was a valley full of people. It was spread out below me like a vast human lake, as though the whole city had emptied and come here. Then I saw a wire fence. Glinting in the dawn light like the steel jaw of a trap, it stretched for as far as the eye could see.

As I descended into the valley, I realised that all these countless people were in fact carefully arranged. Just as with an ants' nest, what you take at first to be chaos soon resolves itself into a pattern. The people were all standing in queues. Each queue led to a different door in a compound of flat-roofed buildings. The longest queue led to the border crossing itself: a roadblock bristling with armed soldiers and razor wire. Somewhere on the other side of this roadblock was the City of Gold, and the promise of hope. Everybody, wherever they were standing, always seemed to be looking in that direction. Surely this was too narrow a gap for so many people.

Trying to keep up my courage, I continued walking down the hill.

It was a forlorn place. The earth was dusty from so many restless feet. The trees had long ago been hacked down for firewood. How could I possibly find one stranger among so many?

The sun grew hotter and hotter as I searched the

hundreds of faces. It was like trying to find a single leaf in the forest. All I could look for was a beard. All I could listen out for, among the deafening din of those hawking food and those arguing, was a single laugh.

The hottest part of the day dropped on us like a great boulder. People wilted, some collapsed. Shadows passed over us. I glanced up – vultures were gathering. Finding a thin piece of shade under a tree with hacked branches, I tried to hide from the worst anger of the sun-man. My thirst hurt, but the heat was too much. It was better to just lie still.

I was drifting home in my thoughts when I felt a tap on the back. It was the girl with red braids. Beckoning she led me through the milling bodies to a water pump. When I had drunk deeply, she handed me a piece of cardboard, showing me how to hold it above my head in order to cast shade. Then, with one last, sad smile, she walked away and was soon lost in the crowd.

Refreshed by the water and the cardboard shade, I began my search again. Gradually I worked my way through the crowd back up the hill to where the bus had set me down. More buses were arriving. People streamed from them like ants. A cold realisation dawned on me: my task was impossible. I might search here for the length of a whole moon and still not find Siana Sulwe.

Yet how could I cross the border without his help? If I really was a cloud then I could float over. But my bare feet were firmly on the ground. Eating more of the bread I came to a decision. Although Peter had said it was dangerous, I was going to try and walk along the fence until I found a way through. Surely it could not stretch forever?

Grandmother, I whispered as I set off, *if ever you walk with me, walk with me now.*

I could not believe it when the old one answered me. Not in my thoughts or in my daydreams but in a real voice. At least I thought it was her calling, so clearly did I hear the voice crying what sounded like: 'Mulumbe! Mulumbe!' Yet when I turned round it was the girl with red braids again. She was telling me something in a language I did not understand. It had only sounded like my name. Once again she was beckoning me. Her smile was welcoming but still sad. For a second time I followed.

'My name is Banyu,' I said in English.

'And my name is Thandi.'

We smiled. We could understand each other. 'Hello, Thandi.'

'Hello, Banyu. You must not go that way. It is too dangerous.'

'There is no other way for me to go.'

'Then come with me.'

She led me back through the crowd and up the hill to where a woman was bending over a cooking pot suspended above a fire. She was blowing on the flames. 'Mother,' said Thandi, 'I have brought the boy who gave me bread.'

Thandi's mother spoke to her daughter in their own language then looked at me. 'Will you eat with us tonight?'

'Thank you,' I replied.

'You are most welcome,' said a man I had not noticed. 'We have heard how you befriended our daughter.' He held out his hand to shake mine. 'Young man, I am Thandi's father.'

The sun was setting when we sat down to eat together. Thandi's parents shared her strange sadness. When they talked in English I was surprised by how much I understood. Thandi's father was a teacher. He said they were not here to cross the border. But he did not explain what else they were doing.

'Sir,' I asked when we had finished eating, 'do you know a man they call Siana Sulwe?'

'No,' he said quickly.

'He has a big . . .' Unable to think of the English word

for a beard I mimed hair growing on a chin. 'And a very loud laugh. You may have heard of him.'

Thandi's father shook his head adamantly. 'I have heard of no man going by that name or description.'

'My child,' Thandi's mother said softly, 'what are you doing here? You are not from this place. We know this by your voice. Do you not realise how dangerous the border is? Are you hoping to cross?'

I shook my head. The fewer people who knew my business the better.

Thandi's father sighed. 'Then you must have come for the same reason as us. Please, sleep with us by our fire. We have a spare blanket.'

'Thank you, Sir,' I replied.

As I lay down, I wondered what had brought Thandi and her family here. They seemed so sad. Did everyone come to the border bearing heavy loads? I slept fitfully. Once when I woke, Thandi's parents were whispering sorrowfully. Although it was still night they had already lit the fire. Other women had risen early too. All over the hill overlooking the border, cooking fires scented the darkness with wood smoke.

It was as I lay there staring at the flickering hillside that I grew aware of a steady tap-tapping. At first I thought it was the sound of vultures digging their beaks into the cold bones of a kill until I realised that it was somebody hammering nails into wood. The sound persisted through the cold, dreary hours of night, multiplying like the calls of the night frogs, until the darkness seemed to be filled with many different hammers calling to each other like living creatures.

The first frail light of dawn revealed the reason for the sound of hammers. A group of men sat nearby, nailing wooden boards together into boxes about the length of a person. The strange heap of their work was already piled high.

We breakfasted to the continued accompaniment of hammering. Thandi's family was now utterly sunk in sorrow. The same desolation seemed to hang over all the families gathered around the growing mound of boxes. Aside from the hammering, all was silent here until a little boy of about Simonje's age came running up the hill from the border crossing. 'They're here!' he cried. 'They're here!'

All the families rose to their feet at the same time. A line of lorries had arrived at the other side of the border. Men were unloading from them. For one instant an even deeper silence closed over everyone like the waters of a mighty lake. Then a scream of anguish rose as though from a single throat.

'They are bringing the lost ones home,' Thandi said.

And with that everyone began to run down the hill. In the surge to reach the border, it was impossible to stand still. Like a branch in a flash flood, I was carried along. 'Where are you going, Thandi?' I called desperately.

'Banyu, my brother has come back.'

'Where has he been?'

'The City of Gold.'

'But this is good news. Why is everyone so sad?'

Reaching the same tree I had sheltered under the previous day, I managed to pull myself from the human flood. Thandi ran on. I quickly lost her in the milling mass of people and the dust they threw up. Her red braids continued to show for a while until they too disappeared. From here I could see the lorries more clearly. Heavy, cumbersome objects were being unloaded. They were the same shape as the boxes.

All at once a sad memory from home visited me. When Grandmother and Namaanza died they had been wrapped in a sheet and laid in the earth. But when our village chief died his body was placed in a box. That box had been the same shape as those made in the night. It had been called a coffin.

By now the crowds were gathering at the crossing point. I was alone on the hillside. Stepping out from the tree, I stared down. 'It is Coffin Friday,' said Thandi's mother suddenly. I had not noticed her standing behind me.

'Coffin Friday?' I asked.

'So many of our people are killed over the border that they return them to us on the first Friday of every month. Do not go to the City of Gold, girl. It is a bad place. Even worse if you are a girl.'

'I am not a girl,' I countered uncertainly.

'You do not need to pretend with me. I heard you talking in your sleep. I think your name is Mulumbe. I think you want to cross the border so that you can go to the City of Gold. But now you see for yourself how those who go to the City of Gold come back. Don't risk your life, Mulumbe.

'I *have* to go.'

'Why?'

I began to tell her about the little ones I had left behind; I began to tell her about the brother I loved; I began to tell her about the night marauders, Olinji, Stepmother . . .

Before I could finish she looked about warily and dropped her voice. 'Yes, Mulumbe. I *have* heard about the man you talked of. The one they call a priest. I did not tell you before because the government punishes those who have anything to do with this Siana Sulwe. You can never be too careful. There are many spies here. But I will try and find him and tell him about you. If you must cross the border, this is the man who might help. I will look for him just as soon as I have brought my son home. Now wait here Mulumbe, and do not ask anyone else about Siana Sulwe. You might be talking to the wrong ears.'

And with that Thandi's mother went down the hill to join the others waiting for their dead to be returned. I sank to the ground.

Body after body was handed over. Once filled, the coffins were hoisted on to shoulders so that they seemed to float on the crowd like terrible boats. One of these death boats caught my eye. Red braids were bobbing beside it. Thandi was bringing her brother home at last.

All at once, I felt as lonely and flightless as a fallen feather. Was Tom still alive; or was this to be his destiny?

CROSSING THE BORDER

Soon all the bodies had gone. And still I waited. 'Mulumbe?' A man was standing above me. 'Are you Mulumbe?' He was speaking my language.

'Yes, Sir,' I replied.

'I am Siana Sulwe.'

For an instant my hopes surged. But then I checked myself. This man had no beard. Getting up, I pulled the cap down over my eyes. 'My name is Banyu,' I announced curtly. 'You have made a mistake.'

The man claiming to be Siana Sulwe looked around shiftily as though he feared he was being watched. Then I heard a sound as welcome as the rain. Throwing his head back he boomed with laughter. 'I suppose you were expecting me to look a little different,' he grinned, stroking his chin.

Still cautious, I asked: 'How do you know my name?'

'I got a message from Thandi's mother. *And* I know your brother.'

'You know, Tom?'

'Yes, now follow me. It's not safe to talk here.'

He led me through the little town that had grown up around the border to a small, single-roomed house made of mud bricks. As soon as he stepped inside the house he closed a pair of curtains then waited anxiously, his body tensed as though the door might be thrust open at any time. I had never seen curtains before. The thin fabric was decorated with the patterns of flowers. At last he sighed with relief. 'We have not been followed. They must still be looking for a man with a beard.' He chuckled. 'I only shaved it off yesterday. In this game we must keep one step ahead. Our government does not take kindly to people helping others to cross the border. But who are you with, girl?'

'I am alone, Sir.'

'You have come from the lake by yourself?' I nodded. He looked at me in surprise. Then began to laugh again. Quietly at first, just a chuckle, then growing slowly like a gathering storm – until the rumbling in his chest broke through a mouth held so wide that it forced his head right back. He did not merely laugh, but thundered. With great relief, I too gave myself up to laughter. It felt as though a drought was breaking deep within me. 'I am glad you are on my side,' he said when we had stopped

laughing at last. 'You would make a formidable enemy.'

'You said you know my brother, Tom, Sir.'

'Even if Thandi's mother had not spoken to me perhaps I would have still recognised you. Tom spoke a great deal about his sister.'

'Is he all right?'

'I will tell you what I know of him. Two boys came to me for help. They were from the lake like you. One of these boys was full of hope; the other seemed close to despair. Only the one full of hope could bring himself to do what was necessary to cross the border. He was your brother. You know, Mulumbe, sometimes I think that the only difference between fear and courage is hope. And never before have I ever met anyone with such hope as your brother.'

'He is safe?'

'We crossed the border safely. When I had to leave him he was still full of hope.' Siana Sulwe studied me with sharp eyes. 'And you, Mulumbe Mudenda, sister of Tom Mudenda, do *you* also want to cross the border? You will have to be braver than you have ever been. I have never helped a girl before –'

'I will do what must be done.'

'Even without knowing what it is?'

'Yes.'

'Your brother was right. There is another Hare walking among us.'

'Sir, people call *you* the Hare.'

'Perhaps that is why we recognised each other. But tell me something, Mulumbe, what would you have done if we had not found each other?'

'I would have found a way across somehow.'

'Yes, I believe you would.'

'Nothing will stop me.'

He gave a low whistle. 'How will our people ever fail when there are young women like you?'

'You too are from the lake, Sir?'

'No, Mulumbe, I am just a citizen of this country, an inhabitant of this continent, a member of the human race. But Tom has told me of your people's story. And I have helped a few others from the lake before. Your history saddens me.'

'They say you are a priest, Sir.'

'Do they?'

'Are you?' I had already asked the question before I realised how disrespectful I was being. Bowing my head, I backed away curtseying.

Gently, he straightened me up. 'No, Hare, now it is for others to show *you* their respect.' He stroked where his beard had been and grinned. 'It is feeling very scratchy

today. I think I will have to grow it back. But to answer your question. Am I a priest? Perhaps I was once. Perhaps I am now. Perhaps in a country like this the little I can do to help people has become the only way I can pray. Mulumbe, now I must go out for a while. There is much to arrange for our crossing. You may have to wait a few days, like your brother did. But you have arrived at a good time. If it could be called that.' He sighed. 'I will explain later.'

Left alone I watched the sunlight pooling against the curtains in the little house. If I concentrated on the pattern hard enough then I could almost block out the unknown ordeal that lay ahead. How could I be so sure that I would be able to do what had so terrified Peter? It must be something too appalling for words.

When Siana Sulwe came back the light at the flowered curtains was beginning to fade, and so was my courage. His words stung me like bees: 'We can go tonight.'

He had brought a little food and as we ate by the light of a candle he spoke about his work. 'I have been shot three times. Once in the arm, once in the leg and once in the shoulder.' He grinned. 'Not a bad trade off. Three bullets for so many lives.'

'You have helped lots of people?'

He waved away the praise. 'There are others whose

part in the work is more important.'

'Now try and get a little sleep. I am afraid you are in for a tough time.'

My voice sounded small in the darkness. 'Siana Sulwe, what is it that I am going to have to do?'

'You will know soon enough.'

I lay in a corner of the room unable to sleep. Siana Sulwe sat in a chair. His silhouette, cast in silver by the moonlight, formed a reassuring shape. The moon-woman was at her fullest. At home now she would be walking over the lake, teasing silver shadows from the trees of the forest . . .

Only a short time seemed to have passed when a soft knock at the door brought Siana Sulwe instantly to his feet. Two men came in. They were carrying something. They put it on the ground. I could not see what it was until Siana Sulwe lit a little candle. 'I am sorry, Mulumbe,' he murmured. 'To cross the border, you must travel in this.'

I stared in disbelief at the long, thin box.

'My child, you must travel in a coffin. This is how we can smuggle you across. You see, not all the dead bodies travel in the same direction across the border. A few days ago one of the people who help us was killed in this country. She was a nun. We buried her at her Mission

Church in the bush, but we have the coffin and the paperwork to take her body down to her Order's Mother House in the City of Gold. Mulumbe, tonight you are going to have to pretend to be her.'

'I am going to have to pretend to be dead?'

'Do not worry about showing lack of respect. It is what she would have wanted. I knew her. She was my friend.' Siana Sulwe broke off for a moment. Pain burnt in his eyes. 'She was killed by the same people who took your mother. Yes, Tom told me all about that.' Siana Sulwe put on a priest's shirt and collar. 'They are more likely to believe that a priest is bringing a nun's body back for burial.'

'Siana Sulwe,' said one of the men, 'we must hurry.'

Nodding, Siana Sulwe turned to me. 'Mulumbe,' he said gently, 'tell me now if this is too much for you. I know the superstitions of many people. Some say that if you lie in a coffin then you will never come out alive. That is why Peter could not do it.'

'I can do it,' I whispered.

'Yes,' he nodded, 'I believe you can.'

One of the men passed him some coloured sticks and he began rubbing them on my face. 'This is make-up. If anyone lifts the lid keep your eyes closed, and they will only see a dead body.'

'Siana Sulwe, we must be going shortly,' the other said.

Siana Sulwe handed me a long, dark blue dress. 'It is a habit,' he explained. 'The nuns wear them. Put it on. And place the other things in your bag. I will look after them for you.'

They turned their backs towards me as I tried to pull on the habit. But it was as though my fingers had become blocks of wood. They would not respond. In the end I had to haul the habit over my head with a pair of fists.

'Now, what is Tom's address?' Siana Sulwe asked. 'Where is he staying?'

'I do not know.'

'You have come all this way without even knowing where to find him? That settles it then. I am going to accompany you. I directed your brother to the house of the nuns where this coffin is supposed to be going. We will try there first.'

'You are coming with me all the way?'

'Yes. If you do not mind.'

I wanted to explain the depth of my gratitude, but could only smile. 'Why do you help us, Sir?'

'Have you ever heard of the story of Honeyguide and the Honeybadger? In a world where no one helps anyone else only the snakes grow fat. Now come on, these gentlemen are putting their lives at risk for us so we must

oblige them. Prepare yourself. You are going to have to stay in the coffin for a long time. Even when you cross the borderline you will not be safe. On the other side you become an illegal alien. The police there will send you back if they catch you. Are you ready?'

Climbing into that coffin was the hardest thing I have ever had to do. No wonder Peter could not do it. I lay flat. Bidding me join my hands together on my chest in a gesture of prayer, Siana Sulwe threaded rosary beads between my fingers. 'There may be some commotion at the border. I do not think they will ask to see the body but if they do then remember: close your eyes and do not move. The border guards will just see a corpse. Now, we are going to have to hammer the lid down.'

How can I describe being sealed in a coffin? All is dark, all feels to be closing in, crushing. It was as though I really had died. The hammer taps reverberated in my head like soil landing on the lid. The rosary beads tightened round my fingers like the roots of a plant. I thought of the poor woman whose place I had taken.

'We are taking you to the truck,' whispered Siana Sulwe as I felt myself being lifted up. 'Knock twice if you think you are going to be all right in there.'

I forced myself to knock. But even as I did so I felt panic rising. It was growing hard to breathe, as though I

was drowning. Was this how my Great Grandfather had felt when the trespassing waters of the lake had sealed themselves above his head? Then all at once, at my moment of greatest need, I was no longer alone. The thought of Great Grandfather burnt like a lamp in the darkness of the coffin. My Grandmother was in here with me too, and all the ancestors. The cry of Fishing Eagle sounded out. Now the lid was as high as the blue sky above the lost river of my people. My breathing began to ease.

I sensed my bearers lifting me on to the back of the truck. Their footsteps receded. 'I am going to drive you to the crossing now,' Siana Sulwe whispered. A few moments later the engine revved and vibrations shook the coffin until I feared that the flimsy boards would fall apart.

I felt every stone and hollow on the way to the checkpoint, but when the wheels beneath me described the smooth stretch of tarmac leading to the roadblock my heart began to beat like a flock of *quelea* finches caught in a bag. The lorry stopped. Voices barked at Siana Sulwe in a language I did not understand. He answered in the same tongue. Then the voices, harsh as those of the night marauders, seemed to explode all around me. The border guards were coming round to the back of the lorry. The bullying sound of their steps told me that they wore army boots.

Now they were so near that I could smell them. It is strange how hate always seems to have the same smell that can penetrate even wood.

The lid suddenly rattled, and I smothered a gasp. Fingernails were scratching at the wood like gnawing rats. They were trying to open the casket. But before they could, Siana Sulwe roared like a lion. 'If you have any fear of God then you will not trouble one of His dead!' The voices shrieked back but their boots were drilling away. 'Mulumbe,' murmured Siana Sulwe, 'listen to me carefully. They have gone to get their superior officer. They want to open the coffin. I will do all I can to stop them but if they lift the lid just close your eyes and do not move.'

How could I keep still? I thought of Hare lying motionless as a piece of firewood to deceive Hyena. But this was no story being told round a fire. A sneeze, an itch, or a single blink would be fatal.

I heard nothing until a soft, sly voice began to talk just above the coffin lid. 'I am sorry, Father,' the man said in English. 'But I must open it. How do I know you are not smuggling diamonds or gold?'

'Smuggling gold to the City of Gold?' Siana Sulwe replied dryly.

'Or guns.'

'Lift the coffin up and you will see there are no weapons inside. It is too light.'

'Father, I am only doing my job.'

'And I am only doing mine. Look it's late. The nuns of our lost sister's congregation will be waiting. A bishop is to officiate at the requiem Mass in the morning. If you hold us up or damage the lid then you will be held responsible.'

'Is that a threat, priest?'

Siana Sulwe's voice fell low. 'I understand, you are just doing your job. Perhaps this will help you to rubber stamp our papers.'

'Are you trying to bribe me, Father?'

'Of course not, I just know how difficult and important your job is. And the paperwork is expensive. A little money might help pay for your time and effort.'

There was a long, terrible silence. Any moment I expected the lid to be yanked off. Then, just when I could bear it no longer, I heard the engine splutter and felt the throbbing vibrations again. My heart flew free as Fishing Eagle hunting above the old river of our people. Once more I had escaped.

We had not gone far into this new country when the vehicle suddenly lurched. The wheels began to bounce

and bump. Had Siana Sulwe lost control of the vehicle just like the driver of Tuff Boy? Then I realised that we had left the relatively smooth surface of the road for a far rougher terrain. Were we driving directly into the bush? The shaking of the coffin throbbed so painfully in my ears that I began to think I would never be able to hear again. Then the motion suddenly stopped. A moment later, the lid of my coffin was being pulled off.

Siana Sulwe was beaming at me. His teeth white as the moon. 'You have done it,' he said.

'Are we there yet, Siana Sulwe?'

'Not yet, child, but we *have* crossed the border. And before we go any further there is something I think you would like to see.'

Unknotting the rosary beads from my clenched fingers, he helped me out of the coffin. Like a new-born gazelle I staggered on unsteady legs.

'Look, Mulumbe,' Siana Sulwe murmured.

I could not understand. He seemed to be pointing out a stretch of open ground where the moon had been caught in a net like a fish.

He smiled at my confusion. 'Mulumbe, this is a river. Not as wide and fast flowing as that which was taken from your people. But still, a river.'

Then I realised that the moon-woman was still free in

the sky and that what I had seen was only her reflection as she peered at herself in the water. 'Ah, a river.'

It was so beautiful, flexing itself like the great leg of a powerful animal. A heady scent filled my nostrils. Not the scent of our lake; this was the enticing fragrance of faraway places brought here on the current, and the promise of vast distances stretching ahead. I peered over the wide, smooth, living reaches. I felt certain that Grandmother was waving at me from somewhere on the other side.

I was still searching for her when the lightning struck. A searing, blinding beam. It did not fade. It was not lightning. 'Quick,' roared Siana Sulwe. 'Get back in the truck.'

'Into the coffin?'

'There's no time, it's the border police! They have caught us in their searchlight.'

But before I could follow him into the lorry, there was a crack of gunfire. The vehicle bucked. 'They have hit the tyres,' cried Siana Sulwe jumping free with my bag. 'Run!'

'Put down any weapon,' a loud voice suddenly boomed. 'You are completely surrounded. Put down any weapon!'

We just managed to make it into a thicket of elephant grass. The stalks all around us danced as another volley of

bullets was fired. 'Quick, don't stop,' Siana Sulwe urged. I pushed deeper and deeper into the dense growth until suddenly I realised that Siana Sulwe was no longer following me. I found him a little way back. He was lying on the ground. His face was clenched with pain. 'What is the matter, Sir?' I asked.

I could hear the border police. Their searchlight raked the thick vegetation.

'Mulumbe,' Siana Sulwe whispered, 'I am sorry to desert you at a time like this but you are going to have to carry on without me.'

The searchlight scoured us. Siana Sulwe was bleeding badly.

'I always knew that it must end this way,' he said. 'The one who lives by dodging Crocodile's jaws will eventually feel his sharp teeth.' He reached for my hand. 'In the City of Gold, look for the Sisters of the Assumption.' He tried to rise but fell back. 'We must stand together now. All people. And with Hare Mulumbe on our side what need we fear?'

'Please do not die, Siana Sulwe.'

'Am I dying? Yes, I suppose I am. It just means I am going to see my friend again. Go now. As for me I have reached the border that all of us must cross alone. Now go. Go, go!'

He closed his eyes. I slipped away through the elephant grass. Behind me the searchlights were blanching the beautiful limb of the river into a bleached bone.

THE COW-DUNG FIRE

Once again I was running from men in the night. But Grandmother was not with me now. The stars above were my only company. The road was bitterly cold beneath my feet. Although I was the one running it seemed to be the night rushing headlong at me. Border police sprang out in the form of trees. Long grass bristled with gun barrels. An owl volleyed over my head like a round of bullets. Even the moon-woman was the searching spotlight of the patrol.

Siana Sulwe had been right. Hope *is* the difference between fear and courage. But where could I find enough hope to carry me on my solitary way? When I had thought that he was coming with me, I believed I could do anything. But now I felt utterly lost.

When my legs would take me no further I changed into Banyu's clothes. Climbing a tree I clung to its branches until dawn. That night lasted a thousand years. I whispered every single story Grandmother had ever told me and invented many new ones. But would I ever be

able to tell the little ones, the tale of how Hare tricked a passage across the border and found his way to the City of Gold?

When dawn came I dropped stiffly from my hiding place and carried on along the dirt road. Hungry and thirsty I was still half-lost in the world of my Grandmother's stories when the miracle happened.

At least that is what I thought it was. A wall of doughnuts blocked my way. Thinking it must be a dream, I closed my eyes. But when I opened them again the doughnuts were as real as ever. I reached out and took one. It was just like the doughnut my father had once bought for me. The same delicious smell, the same little red tongue popping out as I squeezed. And, when I took a bite, the same explosion of taste.

'Hey, what do you think you are doing?' I looked behind me. A boy of about my own age stood there. Beside him was a trolley. 'I got here first,' he challenged. 'The first one to see the horns of the buffalo gets his meat.'

Without replying I finished my doughnut.

His eyes narrowed with curiosity. 'Where are you from?'

Licking my lips, I pointed back down the road.

'Another one from across the border?' His face tightened suspiciously. 'Are you alone, Mr Manchester United?'

'What are you calling me that for?' I demanded.

He pointed at my hat. 'You are wearing a Red Devils cap. Manchester United. A soccer team.'

I grunted. I had heard Tom and Peter talking about soccer teams.

'Are you a Red Devils fan?'

'No,' I returned rudely. 'I am a *tsotsi*.'

'A *tsotsi*?' He stepped back. Fear widened his eyes.

'But my fingers haven't decided whether they wish to steal today.'

'Where are you going, *Tsotsi* Red Devil?'

'Where else? The City of Gold.'

'Ah, Goldi!' He gazed at me with respect. 'Why are you going there?'

'To get rich,' I boasted.

No longer so sure of himself the boy watched me as I gobbled another doughnut. 'Are you going to eat *all* the doughnuts?'

'Maybe.'

'They dropped from a truck this morning. Trucks always skid on this corner. No one else knows about them yet. Manchester United, if you like we could work together. In return I will give you proper food. You will be sick if you eat only doughnuts.'

'I suppose I could help,' I replied and still chewing,

began to stack the doughnuts on to his trolley. 'Now for business,' he declared, setting off down a sandy track into the bush. I followed, steadying the stack of doughnuts, helping to lift the trolley over rocks, picking up any that fell.

The earth was dusty, exhausted. Most of the big trees had been cut down. Here and there cattle stared at us. As we went along my new companion picked up pieces of their dung and placed them on the trolley too.

After a while some huts came into view. It was a huge village, bigger than even the district centre. The boy suddenly stopped. 'What's in your bag?'

'A blanket,' I replied, reaching into the bag to touch the blanket Siana Sulwe had given me.

'Can I borrow it, Manchester United? Strictly for business purposes.'

I handed it over. The boy quickly covered his haul.

'Just in time,' he said.

A crowd of young children were running towards us. 'Hey, Bhuti!' they shouted. 'What you got on your trolley today?'

'Nothing for you babies.'

'But what is your business today?'

'Just dung,' he replied.

'We don't believe you. What's under that blanket?'

'I'm telling you, it's dung.'

'Bhuti, who's that with you?' they asked.

'A *tsotsi*.'

We hurried on. Laughing and shrieking, more and more children followed us until our trolley was wagging a long tail of laughter and shouting. 'Hey, are you really a *tsotsi*?' they called at me.

'*And* he's a devil,' Bhuti said.

Those nearest to me danced away.

'Watch out,' Bhuti laughed. 'If you don't leave us alone he'll grab you!'

We came to a busy road lined with many stalls. Carpenters selling carved animals. Barbers shaving heads. Cooks vending hot food. There were countless other things for sale. Fruit, leather belts, little buses crafted from wire, model hens fashioned from plastic bags. Cars stopped constantly, their drivers and passengers coming out to browse at the roadside market.

'What you got, Bhuti man?' the other traders asked. With a flourish he pulled back the blanket. Carefully concealing the dung, he revealed the doughnuts. There were whistles of admiration. 'Where did you get those jammy beauties from?'

Bhuti pointed at me. 'Meet my supplier, but watch out, he's from the City of Gold. Just look at his cap – David Beckham gave it to him personally.'

In a loud voice Bhuti began to tout for customers: 'Lovely delicious doughnuts,' he cried. 'Red Devil specials. So nice they want to eat themselves. For one day only. Eat yours, before somebody else does.'

Our stock quickly shrank. Bhuti put the notes and coins into a pouch tied tightly round his waist. 'Hey Manchester United,' he laughed, 'you've brought me luck. This is the best day I've ever had.' And still the customers came. 'You wait here, and sell what is left,' he said. 'I'll take the trolley and get the rest.'

After he'd gone a white person came to our stall. I had only ever seen white people from a distance.

Her eyes were blue as the sky. Her long, straight hair red as a sunset. Her face so white that it dazzled me. It was as though the moon-woman herself had come down to be our customer. I remembered what Siana Sulwe had said. No matter how strange she looked we were all *members of the same human race*. She bought a doughnut. As she handed the money over I noticed that her arms were speckled with freckles, like the hide of a buck fawn.

Bhuti came back without the trolley. 'The others have found them,' he sighed, but he cheered up when he counted his money. Only the smearings of jam and a few crumbs were left on the ground at our feet. And they too began to disappear as a legion of ants marched away with

them. 'Come, Manchester United. We have done well. Business was good. The best for a long time. Now let us eat some proper food.' As we walked he studied me through the corner of his eye. 'Are you really a *tsotsi*?'

I shook my head.

He took me to a hut. An old man was squatting over a cow-dung fire.

'Grandfather,' Bhuti said, 'this boy has come from across the border.'

The old man did not look up. Taking a fresh piece of dung, he placed it on the fire and blew it into flames. His cheeks rose and fell like bellows so that one moment he looked full faced, the next skeletal. When a thin finger of smoke finally rose, a smile cracked the old face.

'Grandfather,' said Bhuti, 'this boy is going to Goldi.'

The old man stirred the pot that hung above the fire. The food smelt delicious. As Bhuti and I waited for it to cook I wondered when Magoyela and the others would next sit round a full cooking pot. That would only happen if I could reach the City of Gold.

'Manchester United,' Bhuti said, 'are the villages in your country empty? So many of you pass through here on your way to the City of Gold.'

'Many pass through here?'

'Nearly every day.'

'Tell me. Have you seen a young man called Tom Mudenda?'

'Tom Mudenda?'

'He is my brother. He too went to the City of Gold, to Goldi. I am searching for him.'

Bhuti shrugged. 'So many pass through we no longer notice them.'

I sighed. It was not going to be that easy finding Tom.

The soup we ate was flavoursome and nourishing. Then I was handed a gourd to drink from. It was milk, but not given by goats. Richer, thicker, it melted down my throat like honey. It was milk from a cow.

After our meal, Bhuti led me back to the busy road. He opened his money pouch and held out some notes. 'Your share, partner. Enough to get to Goldi. A bus stops over there.'

'Thank you.'

I had walked a little way when he called after me: 'Sizwe Sibanda.'

I turned.

'Sizwe Sibanda,' he repeated. 'Maybe when you are searching for Tom Mudenda you will also find Sizwe Sibanda. Tell him we are waiting for him here. He is my father. He left a year ago.'

'Sizwe Sibanda,' I said, nodding

Bhuti's face was filled with longing. 'Tell him we are waiting for him to come home. Tell him about my trolley. Tell him we could go into business with it. He will not have to go away again.'

And with that he disappeared back down a sandy path, searching for something else to transport to the market on his trolley.

I had to wait a long time for a bus to come. We drove through the night. In my dreams a gun was being fired. Somebody fell under the bullets. I ran over to him, thinking that it was Siana Sulwe, but found instead the face of my brother.

THE CITY OF GOLD

Nothing could have prepared me for the City of Gold. I woke to find myself in the heart of an ants' nest. And somebody had just been stirring it.

Completely surrounded by jostling people and cars, our bus had slowed to little more than walking pace. Sounding his horn and yelling out of the window constantly, the driver jerked us forward by fits and starts. I could not bear to look. Any moment someone was surely going to be crushed beneath our wheels. But before this could happen, the bus just seemed to give up. Its engine gasped and it shuddered to a halt. Everyone on board stood up.

Stepping off the bus into the frenzy of bodies and vehicles, the cold hit me like a punch. It was still early morning.

'Who are you pushing, boy?' someone demanded.

'Don't bang into people,' another said, elbowing me.

'How can you be drunk so early?' A third shoved me aside.

I dodged away from the hostile faces only to see a car heading straight towards me. There was no time to jump free. I closed my eyes. The tyres screeched. I waited. So this is it, I thought, I have come so far only to fail now. But I was not hit by the car, only by a yelling voice. When I opened my eyes I saw that the car had stopped a hand's width from me. 'What's the matter?' the driver shrieked. 'Life not sweet enough for you?'

The car disappeared into the crowd but hardly was there time to recover when a deafening blare of horns scattered the pedestrians. A cavalcade of minibuses was bulldozing its way through the congestion. Each one of the battered vehicles was crammed with passengers. Arms and legs waved through the open windows as though the minibuses were pythons and had swallowed their passengers.

It was utter confusion: the dizzying stench of exhaust fumes, the horns and engines of the vehicles, the throbbing mass of pushing people. When a herd of buffalo stampedes, it does not stop to think what might be crushed beneath its hooves. A human herd is no different.

Many of the women carried loads on their heads: huge bunches of bananas, bags stuffed to the seams, boxes pounding out music, even suitcases. The loads teetered dangerously, threatening to fall on me each time one of their bearers pushed past. When a momentary gap in the throng of bodies showed a sandy track leading off the main road, I took my chance. Calling on Banyu, I began to push through the bodies, swimming against the flow of elbows, legs and cars.

Bumped and bruised, I managed at last to reach the track. Without looking back I hurried along. But what I saw now, as the track climbed, disorientated me even more. My first view of the City of Gold.

I had never expected it to be anything like this. It stretched for as far as the eye could see. But it was not made of gold. Nothing gleamed, everything seemed drab, dirty. Even the air itself was gritty with smog. If everyone had come here looking for riches, no one seemed to have found any yet. On every available piece of land shacks sprouted. Some of them were constructed of dried mud, wooden boards or tarpaulin. But many were little more than a piece of plastic sheeting stretched over poles. The early morning sun glinted off countless corrugated-iron roofs on which perched peculiar metal shapes. It seemed to me that a vast flock of strange vultures had gathered, waiting for a disaster. Only later would I come to know them as television aerials.

Where on earth could I begin to search for my brother?

The path took me through tight streets of shacks,

carried me over an open patch of ground where women with babies on their backs scavenged through ankle-deep rubbish, and then almost threw me into a little river.

There was nothing beautiful about *this* river. Thick with bobbing cans, bottles and excrement, a terrible stench rose from the water. The rotting body of a dead dog floated by at my feet. A little way downstream I saw where the main road would have taken me. A great crowd of people had massed on the bank where two wooden planks and a fallen tree were the only ways across the stinking current. Everybody was pushing and shoving to cross these precarious bridges. As I watched, one of the struggles flared into violence. The sun caught the eye of a glinting knife. The crowd melted away from the blade. There was shouting, kicking, then a splash. A human body now floated beside the carcass of the dog.

Hiding in a thicket of sickly-looking eucalyptus trees that grew close by, I scanned the crowd crossing the plank and trunk bridges. Perhaps Tom was one of those jostling to get over. But I would never find him this way. It would be like trying to find a single leaf in the forest. I needed to locate the Sisters of the Assumption but whom could I stop and ask for directions? Only the unwise approached strangers in the City of Gold. The click of a knife was the mother tongue of this place. Hare had to outwit a handful of enemies. I was up against a whole city.

Then all at once the vast flood of people ebbed. The queue at the unsteady bridges thinned. Emerging from the trees I hurried over one of the flimsy crossings. Downstream, lines of washing hung between the trunks of the riverside trees. Even here, by a polluted, flooding stream, people had built their homes. Feeling a heel sink into the foul water, I scrambled on to the far bank and continued on my way.

The dusty tracks between the endless shacks were quieter now. Those left behind were just waking. A few sat outside their shacks, yawning and stretching as they chatted with each other. Without the cover of the crowds I felt conspicuous, like a mouse having to leave the shelter of the grass to cross bare earth. Skirting a body lying in the middle of the track, I remembered the sleeping logs of Four Wheels' city. The smell rising from this man told me that he was not dead, just drunk. I did not wait to see if he would wake up.

I had been walking through the maze of shacks for what felt like hours when I saw something that made my heart soar above all this seething confusion: a building with a huge cross on its side. I had found a church. Surely they would be able to help me find the Sisters of the Assumption. Everything was going to be all right.

Reaching through a metal grille, I knocked. There was no answer. I knocked again. Still no one seemed to hear me. A third, even louder attempt brought no response. Gathering all my courage I pressed my face against the grille and called out: 'Hello, is there anyone there?'

The door began to open. 'Pastor is praying,' said a face peering through the metal bars.

'Please, I am looking for someone.'

'Pastor will be a *very* long time. He has souls to save.'

'His name is Tom Mudenda.'

The face's hard eyes scrutinised me; I did not know if they belonged to a man or a woman. 'Are *you* saved, child?'

'Siana Sulwe helped him, and he saved me.'

'Saved you? No. Only the Lord can save you.'

'Please,' I begged, 'do you know where I can find the Sisters of the Assumption?'

'Sisters?' The eyes narrowed with suspicion. 'Do you mean nuns?'

'Yes. My brother went to them. Tom Mudenda. They might know where –'

'Come closer and tell me his name again.'

I stepped forward but before I could repeat my brother's name a hand whipped through the grille and caught me by the neck. The fingers were thin but strong, and tightened round my throat like the noose of a snare. 'Amen! I have caught this child for you. Another fish is in the net. Amen! Amen!' I could not move. The face opened its mouth in triumph as though to swallow me. 'Do not struggle, boy. This is your salvation.'

I could hardly breathe.

The grille opened and a second hand shot out. Twisting my head I bit the wrist. There was a scream, the grip slackened for a second. I pulled away.

'You have bitten the hand of the Lord,' the face screamed after me as I ran. 'You nail of Golgotha! Go, go to your nuns! Go to your spawn of the devil. You will find only madness and sin there.'

No matter how far I ran the terrible face seemed to pursue me, its wide mouth ready to bite and eat.

All day I searched the tracks running between endless shacks. Once, as I queued to drink from a public tap, I thought I caught sight of my brother. Forgetting my thirst I ran after him. 'Tom, Tom!' I cried. 'It's me, Mulumbe.'

But it was not my brother. I had lost my place in the water queue. I had to begin at the back of the line again.

The sun was beginning to set when I found myself beside the stinking, little river once more. Where could I go? Without warning the crowds from the morning returned. Quickly I hid myself in the same thicket of forlorn trees and watched the heaving mass of humanity.

There were no red fires of sunset in the City of Gold. Here the day just choked itself to death and the night smeared the sky like oil leaking from an engine.

At home the fireflies would be rising in search of the stars. The only stars twinkling here were the little bulbs of the endless shacks. I had broken my promise to Peter. Night had fallen and I was in the City of Gold. Alone.

MAMA SIKELELE, THE SHEBEEN QUEEN

If up to now the City of Gold had been like a hyena, with the coming of night it became a leopard. Jumping down from its fork in the tree, it stretched, yawned and began to prowl.

Picking my way through the seething night, I hoped only to go unnoticed. Loud music throbbed from every corner of the sprawling township, its pulse seeming to grow more and more rapid – like the quickening heart of a hunter. The shacks shook with singing and shouting. Groups of men straddled the middle of the road drinking. Couples danced drunkenly. *Tsotsis* lurked in doorways like night adders waiting for an unsuspecting foot. Gunfire snarled. Sirens wailed: restless ghosts haunting the makeshift streets.

When two people fell brawling across my path, I only just managed to dart into one of the many shadows and slip past. If I continued roaming the streets like this, something told me I would not last the night. I had to find a hole deep enough to crawl into.

I turned down a narrower, darker track. There was no electricity here. Instead lanterns stared out from the shacks, like leopards' eyes. All the same it felt safer in the shadows. No wonder so many animals are nocturnal. The night can be the friend of the weak.

Coming across a piece of corrugated iron leaning against a wall, I looked around. No one else seemed to be near. There were no lights close-by, no voices. All I could hear was the barking of a faraway dog and the thudding of distant music. I crawled in behind the sheet of metal.

It was only now that I realised just how cold it was. Even under my blanket I was shivering. I put on Mutinta's dress over Banyu's clothes, but the fingers of the night still penetrated me. Soon I could not feel my fingers and feet. I tried to bear it but even my lips grew numb. I crept from the hiding place. It was still quiet. Flapping my arms, I began to jump on the spot. Higher and higher, just like Peter and Tom on the night of honey, but there was no joy in my movements. I danced only to get some feeling back in my limbs so that I could hide again.

I did not notice the man watching me until he laughed drunkenly. The familiar stench of sour beer hit me like a zebra kick. I stared back, trying to scowl like Banyu but then I realised Banyu had been covered by Mutinta's dress.

'Hello, darling,' he crooned. 'I like your frock.'

He lurched forward. I dodged just in time and sprinted away. But I didn't get far. Another man had materialised. 'Hey, baby, why dance by yourself when I am here!'

Coiling myself free from the hands digging into my arms like thorns, I ran towards the music and lights. Surely someone would help me. But turning a corner I found it was a dead end.

The wreck of a burnt-out car lay close by. I threw myself behind it and waited. Perhaps they were so drunk that they had forgotten about me. But I was not to be so lucky. A few moments passed, then I heard them coming.

'Baby, you still want to dance?' one of them sang.

'Where are you, sweetheart of mine?' the second crooned.

'My princess, I am ready for you,' another giggled.

There were three of them and no escape. I looked wildly about but only found a pair of terrified eyes watching from one of the shack windows. Even as I appealed to the eyes, they disappeared. The men were now approaching the car.

At the last possible moment I sprang over the wreck, hoping to create an instant's surprise; my foot caught in

the dress and I was sent sprawling across the ground. There was a whoop of drunken laughter. But before the men could grab me, something clicked. I turned. The door of the shack where the terrified eyes had been watching now stood ajar. Jumping up, I ran inside.

A young woman stood in the shack holding a baby. She pointed at an open door in the other wall. With a grateful smile, I slipped through. She closed it quickly behind me.

I found myself on a long, straight thoroughfare. Racing away I stopped only when my breath gave out. Chest heaving, I turned round. I had lost my pursuers. I waited for a while just to make sure they had not come after me, then carried on.

The relief was short-lived. Turning a corner, I saw that two of the men were waiting for me. The third one slipped from an alley behind me, cutting off my escape.

It was the stench of sour beer that seemed to grab at me as much as their hands. They had pinioned me from behind. Two people passed by. I screamed at the top of my lungs. The passers-by hurried on in terror. 'Relax, princess,' the first man soothed.

'Why not have a drink and enjoy yourself?' the second coaxed.

'Float on wings, girl,' the third murmured.

All three of the men crushed around me. It felt as though I'd been swallowed and lay tight in the belly of a living thing.

At that moment I heard the loudest shout I have ever heard. My attackers froze. Dropping me to the ground, they backed away. Utterly dazed, I could not even crawl away. The shout continued to grow louder and louder. The men tried to scatter. But it was too late. A woman stood in their way. A long, traditional robe rippled from her body; her headdress towered over my assailants.

She threw one of them over her shoulder as though he was nothing more than a sack of mealie meal. The second she simply forced to the ground. Picking themselves up these two scuttled away. It was the smallest one that she really wanted.

'Oh Mama Sikelele, how are you on this beautiful night?' the small man grovelled. 'You laughing at our little joke?'

'Come here.' The woman's soft tone contrasted with her clear power, in the same way that a lioness contracts her claws in a velvet paw.

'Don't tell me you thought we were going to hurt her, Mama Sikelele. Look, she's all right.' My assailant's voice shook like a kid goat as he pointed at me.

Mama Sikelele continued to beckon, her voice still quiet. 'Come to Mama Sikelele.'

'Listen, Mama. Ask the girl, she'll say we didn't –' He bent down to pick me up.

'You get off her!' The soft voice held only the hint of a growl. 'And come here.'

Cringing with fear the man approached. Mama Sikelele stared deep into his eyes. 'This is what Mama Sikelele say to you. She say, you come round here one more time then she gonna give you more than this –'

'Please, Mama Sikelele, don't hurt me! Don't hurt –' the man whimpered as Mama Sikelele reached out and grabbed his arms.

She lifted him clear from the ground before tossing him away. He landed with a grunt, then, still whimpering, dragged himself away like a spider with a broken leg. I watched him until he had gone from view. When I looked back Mama Sikelele had gone too. And the crowd that had gathered was already melting away.

I tried to get up but could not. The dust at my feet was wet with my own tears. My body ached where the hands had bruised my flesh. My lungs felt like chewed mealie cobs. But it was my inner heart that hurt the most. All hope was gone. Only fear was left and it claimed me like flies on a carcass. I had got this far, but would go no

further. The river inside me had been dammed. Abject in the dust, I had failed Siana Sulwe. I had failed everyone.

'Why you cry, girl?'

I did not even bother to look up at the person speaking. I was spent, paralysed. Like a burnt stick, I would never feel warmth again.

'It takes fewer muscles to laugh than to cry.'

'Leave me alone,' I whispered.

'I can't leave alone a bird with a broken wing.'

And with those words I felt myself being lifted from the ground. 'Mama Sikelele, she say no more crying now, girl.' I opened my eyes. I was looking in the face of an African queen. Those hands which had beaten up my assailants, were now gentle as a mother's. Mama Sikelele smiled. 'Come home with me, child.' The instinct that lies deep in all living things whispered that at last I was safe.

Mama Sikelele carried me over the threshold of a corrugated iron door then through a dark, smoky room full of people. Drunken voices rose and fell. Music blasted out. Cigarettes glinted. I lurched with fear but then realised that people were making way for my rescuer. 'Hey, Mama Sikelele!' they greeted her.

'You sort out the bad men, Mama Sikelele?'

'I'm glad it's not me you tangling with, Mama Sikelele.'

Her response was a single, regal nod of the head.

Another door took us down a long, narrow passage at the bottom of which was a quiet room. Here she laid me on a bed, whispering: 'Mama Sikelele, she say welcome to my home-sweet-home.'

I don't know how many days I lay ill on that bed feverishly drifting in and out of consciousness. My sleeping moments were strange nightmares: the distorted faces and voices of those I had encountered on my journey, the suffering eyes of those I had left behind. My waking hours were just as unreal, but they brought me happiness. Whenever I woke, Mama Sikelele was either mopping my brow, trying to make me drink soup or bouncing a baby in her arms. I loved to watch her crooning a lullaby to the baby. It was like watching a lioness with her cub. And sometimes as I watched them, I thought I was watching my own mother nursing me.

I began to feel better. Mama Sikelele told me about herself. She was what they called a *Shebeen Queen*. The room of milling bodies she had brought me through was her drinking den. The baby was her daughter. She was called Message. And when I was strong enough I would be able to hold her.

The bruises the attackers had left on my body quickly began to fade. But those on my heart took longer.

Although the days were improving, nightmares still stalked my sleep. I could not bring myself to answer Mama Sikelele's questions about my parents or talk about the journey.

Sometimes at night when Mama Sikelele sat with me and Message, there would be a commotion in the *shebeen*. Without hurrying she would go down the passage. Her shout thundered out then there would be calm. It was on one of these occasions that I noticed she kept a gun hidden in the depths of her traditional robes. Coming back from the drinking den she had not put it back properly. She saw me looking at it. 'Ah, girl,' she murmured sadly, 'to keep safe in the City of Gold even Mama Sikelele, she need a little help.'

Through the long days and nights of my recovery she sat on the side of the bed and told me about the City of Gold and how it got its name. It was full of people who had come for the riches everyone talked about. But all they found were the goldmines: the deepest, cruellest places in the world. 'So deep,' Mama Sikelele said, 'that they swallow all our hopes and yet never seem to be full. And if you fall down them, there is no way back up again.'

'Have you always lived here, Mama Sikelele?' I asked.

'Sometimes I think I have,' she replied. 'But I came

here first with my father. I was a girl of about your age. My father died in one of the mines.'

'Ah, what did you do then?'

'I worked as a maid in one of the big houses owned by the white people.'

I returned her trust and slowly began to tell her about my journey. One by one I named the little ones I had left at home. 'And it was for them that I had to come, Mama Sikelele.'

'You came all that way alone?' she asked in disbelief.

'Do you think my brother is working in a goldmine?'

'Maybe, Mulumbe. Maybe not. Just as everybody has their own reason for coming to the City of Gold, everybody must find their own fate.'

'Do you have a husband?' I asked her one morning after I managed to dress myself and walk around the room for the first time. A strange look came over her. 'I'm sorry, I did not mean to pry.'

She remained quiet for a few moments then burst into laughter. 'Who say Mama Sikelele need a husband? She a *shebeeny queeny*!'

With returning strength I helped Mama Sikelele to clean the shebeen at the quietest time in the morning. I would fill the cooking pot too, but more than anything I loved playing with Message. Pressing my cheek against

hers, as I had seen Mama Sikelele do, I would breathe in the warm aroma of love while telling her about the little ones I had left behind. 'In the language of the River People my name is Message too,' I would whisper to her over and over.

Often I told her Grandmother's stories. Mama Sikelele would listen too, her eyes growing wide at the dangers facing Hare; her laughter as loud as any child's at his daring escapes.

'Mulumbe,' Mama Sikelele said one day, 'it is time for you to continue your search.'

I hung my head. 'Mama Sikelele, I am too frightened.'

'So what you going to do, girl? Stay here and play *shebeeny queeny* with me?' She reached into her robe and brought out the gun. '*Yebo*, girlie, you stay here and you will have to learn how to make this baby talk. Listen to Mama Sikelele when she speak. A brother is better than a gun.'

The sun welcomed us as we passed through the corrugated-iron door and into the daylight. Mama Sikelele wore her usual African robes. Message gurgled and giggled on her back. I too had been given flowing robes and a headdress to wear. Mama Sikelele nodded as she looked at me: 'You and me, Mulumbe, we a real queen and princess.

A royal family. Now, let us go and see these Sisters of the Assumption. At last I have been able to find an address.'

'Mama Sikelele,' I burst out. 'At the other church they said that nuns are full of madness and sin.'

'Girl,' she said, roaring with laughter, 'and who isn't?'

It was so different walking through the township with Mama Sikelele. Nobody jostled us. Even though it was the busiest time both people and traffic seemed to give her a wide berth. At the little river everybody made way for us to pass over the plank bridge first. When she stepped in front of one of the minibuses, it was the driver who apologised: 'Hey, Mama Sikelele,' he cried. 'I see you!' He lifted his hand out of the window and Mama Sikelele slapped it resoundingly in greeting.

'I see you too, Bloke Boy,' she replied smiling.

'And who is this delightful girl at your side?'

Mama Sikelele winked at me. 'She my daughter, up from the country.'

'Daughter? Sister you mean!'

Chuckling, he opened the door and we both got in his vehicle. 'Where to, my lovely *shebeeny queenies*?'

She gave him some directions and he set off again negotiating the thick traffic. He grinned at me in the mirror. 'Hey, younger sister. There's no finer woman than Mama Sikelele.'

'I know!' I replied with a grin. Bloke Boy was the kind of person to tease a sad mouth into a smile, to twist a smile into a laugh.

'Younger sister?' His eyes sparkled in the mirror. 'Will you ask Mama Sikelele something for me?' I nodded. 'This is what Bloke Boy wants to know: if he asks her, will Mama Sikelele turn Bloke Boy down again?'

'Ask her what?'

'She know. *Yebo*, she know!'

Nudging me, Mama Sikelele pretended to frown. 'Mama Sikelele,' she said, 'she sick of telling Bloke Boy. She not marrying no one. Anyway, how does Bloke Boy know she not married already?'

But Bloke Boy was not giving up. 'Hey, younger sister, tell your older sister this. Mama Sikelele, she like a country chief. She can marry more than one. No finer woman than Mama Sikelele. Younger sister, Bloke Boy fell in love the first day he saw her.'

Horns bellowed at us. 'Let Bloke Boy forget marriage and remember his driving!' laughed Mama Sikelele.

Gradually the cars on the road became newer and shinier. Then the streets quietened. No rubbish littered them. Rising from behind tall walls topped with razor wire, the houses, painted white against the sun, grew bigger and bigger. So *this* was where the gold was to be

found. 'Stop right here,' Mama Sikelele suddenly ordered.

The screech and stench of burning rubber filled the air as Bloke Boy complied. For a while Mama Sikelele sat staring through the window at the beautiful street. 'Mama Sikelele's dream,' whispered Bloke Boy. 'This is where her *shebeen*'s going to take her.'

'Hush now,' urged Mama Sikelele, but her eyes were widening

Bloke Boy nodded. 'When Mama Sikelele work round here as a girl, she make herself a promise. One day she gonna live here. But how she earn the money for one of these palaces? Only by opening a *shebeen*. That's the only way for a good woman to make money in the City of Gold.'

'How much you asking for your fare?' Mama Sikelele demanded.

He waved away her money. 'Put it towards your palace!'

We got out. 'You drive off now!' Mama Sikelele commanded Bloke Boy. 'Mama Sikelele not want you hanging about the place making it look untidy.' The vehicle disappeared and still we had not moved. I saw uncertainty in Mama Sikelele's eyes. She was the undisputed queen of the township but this was not her kingdom.

*

From the pavement we could no longer see the houses. Just their tall walls from which a jumble of signs and pictures glared down at us. 'What are they?' I asked.

'They are warnings, Mulumbe.' She pointed to each sign in turn. '*Armed response unit!* That means someone will shoot you if you try and climb the wall. *Passop Vir die hond!* Look out for the savage dog. *Qhaphela inyoka!* The worst of all: beware of the poisonous snake.'

The wire on top of the wall was sharper than acacia thorns. It crackled with electricity. 'Is it because of the gold?' I asked.

'What gold?'

'That lies on the other side of these walls.'

'Yes,' she said. 'It is because of the gold. Now come on.'

An armed security guard watched us from a patrol box. As we passed him, his dog leapt at us. Only the chain stopped it from savaging our skin. The barking was taken up by other dogs in the vicinity so that it sounded like a whole pack was baying for our blood.

'Here we are.' Stopping at some high gates, Mama Sikelele pressed a button on a little box. There was a pause then: 'Hello, who is it?' a voice asked from the box.

I jumped back in shock.

Mama Sikelele cleared her throat. 'We are looking for a boy, a young man,' she explained to the box.

'There are no boys here. This is a convent of sisters.'

'He is called Tom Mudenda. We were told you might know where he is. He was helped by the one they call Siana Sulwe.'

'You know Siana Sulwe?' the voice demanded hungrily. 'Who are you?

Mama Sikelele motioned me to speak. 'Just talk into the box,' she whispered. 'Tell them everything you know.'

'I am Mulumbe Mudenda.'

'Do you know Siana Sulwe?'

'He helped me.'

'When did you last see him?'

I hesitated. 'We crossed the border together.'

There was a loud buzzing and the gates sprang open. A nun appeared. She wore the same habit that I had worn in the coffin. To see it again made me shudder. 'My name is Sister Mary-Agnes. Please come in.'

Taking me by the hand Sister Mary-Agnes led us down a long, long corridor. It made me think of the path through the forest to the *Sikatonga*'s hut. She walked quickly. I could tell by the energy of her grip that she wanted to run. Pictures of Jesus and Mary looked down at us from the walls as we passed door after door. At last she stopped at one of the doors, and opened it.

In the room we entered, books lined the walls – too many to count. The ground was covered with soft rugs and my feet sank into them as though I was standing in the shallows of the lake. When I sat in a chair, I seemed to float in the air like a butterfly hovering round the *munimbwa* flower. Through a window I saw the spire of a church rising to heaven. The nun had picked up a phone. Mama Sikelele gave Message the breast. Despite my almost unbearable tension, the sound of contented feeding seemed to calm the room.

Sister Mary-Agnes spoke excitedly. Her voice filled the beautiful room like the fluttering of a little bird. As I listened to her my thoughts blurred. One moment she seemed to be talking about Siana Sulwe, the next about Tom Mudenda. 'Yes,' she said finally. 'He is her brother.'

When she put the phone down, she smiled at me. But the smile was quickly replaced by worry. 'Mulumbe, what has happened to Siana Sulwe?'

I could not speak. Sorrow for Siana Sulwe took away my words. My need to know about Tom made me want to scream.

'She crossed the border about three weeks ago,' Mama Sikelele explained for me.

'Yes, we heard she was coming. Siana Sulwe rang to tell

us to expect her. But we have not heard from him since. We did not know what had happened.' Hope flashed across Sister Mary-Agnes's face. 'Where is he, child?'

I felt sick within.

'He is a friend of ours. Siana Sulwe,' the nun said. 'A very precious friend.'

'He was a friend of mine too,' I whispered.

Sister Mary-Agnes's voice dropped. 'You say *was*? Has he been arrested? Mulumbe, you are the last person to have seen him. Please tell us where you last saw him.'

'S-sister,' I stuttered.

'What is it, child?'

'Siana Sulwe is dead. I left him on the bank of a river.'

A single tear ripped its way down the sister's cheek like a thorn. 'I knew it,' she whispered in a torn voice. 'In my heart of hearts, I knew it. He was a saint, you know.'

I nodded.

'It could not have ended any other way. He knew the risks but still took them.'

Flicking away her tears she came and sat beside me. 'But now is not a moment for sorrow. Now is the moment for which our Siana Sulwe gave his life. Now is the time for joy and a celebration of his life.'

Just then the handle in the door turned. A young man came in. He hovered at the threshold. Aware of the nun's

sorrow beside me I only glanced at him wondering why he had interrupted us. But then I looked again. What I saw now made me jump to my feet. I had found the one leaf in the forest. 'Tom!' I cried. 'Is that really you, Tom?'

'Mulumbe!' he replied as though he too had just recognised me. We could barely speak. He gestured at my headdress. 'You look like a princess.'

I gazed at my brother, even as he laughed he was screwing his eyes tight against the tears. 'No,' I whispered, 'let the tears flow as well as the joy. Those tears will carry us both back home.'

'Mulumbe,' he gasped. 'I thought you were dead. My letter to you and Peter must have reached the village just after you left . . . Then when Peter wrote telling me about Olinji . . . and when we heard from Siana Sulwe that he was bringing you . . . and you never came . . . and . . .' He shuddered then smiled in his tears. 'I promise you this now, my sister, you will never have to live with either Olinji or Stepmother again.'

Our embrace was as deep as the river that gave our people its name. And as I closed my eyes I saw Grandmother standing on the far bank. Her arms were stretched out like the drowned trees. She was beckoning me, calling us back. And at that moment, although it would not be easy,

I *knew* we would return to our village. I knew that once again, I would sit round the fire with the little ones, with Peter, with Tom. Then when everyone had eaten well, and the sky bulged with its countless silver stars like the fishing nets of God, I would begin to tell the remarkable story of Hare's dangerous journey to the City of Gold, his many narrow escapes and his safe return. After stories, we would play a game of riddles. Already I saw myself searching in the flames for a good puzzle as Grandmother always did, before beginning with these words: *Who am I? I am a cloud, I can blow anywhere . . .*

AUTHOR'S NOTE AND GLOSSARY

I am a cloud, I can blow anywhere is a work of fiction but it draws its inspiration from the Tonga people of Zimbabwe and Zambia. The Tonga are known for their fine skill in arts and crafts, but perhaps the greatest gift they have to give to the world is their huge knowledge of nature. They can find food and medicine in countless places; they know the secrets of the earth that we, in our technological blindness, have forgotten.

We have used the Tonga name for some of the plants and animals encountered in the pages of this book. We believe that it gives the story a more authentic feel, as well as demonstrating the rich musical quality of this beautiful language. For the same reason we have used Tonga greetings.

GREETINGS

The Tonga people have a range of different greetings
that are made depending on the time of day, and
who is speaking to whom.

* *Wabuka (biyeni)*: Good morning, used by all age groups to young people. Literally: *How did you wake up?*
* *Mwabuka (biyeni)*: Good morning, used by the young when speaking to older people to show respect. Literally: *How did you wake up?*
* *Wayusa (biyeni)*: Good afternoon, used by all age groups to young people. Literally: *How did you spend your day?*
* *Mwayusa (biyeni)*: Good afternoon, used by young people when speaking to older people. Literally: *How did you spend your day?*
* *Kwasiya (biyeni)*: Good evening. Literally: *It is dark now.*

To reply to these greetings you can say *iyii* to show
agreement, or repeat the greeting adding *biyeni*.

GLOSSARY OF TERMS

❀ *bubalubalu wood*. The branches of the *bubalubalu* tree are tied together in bundles. During the evening the bundles are taken to termite mounds and lit. Attracted by the light of the flames the termites fly up. The Tonga can then catch them: a vital source of protein in their diet.

❀ *bula bird*. This Woodland Kingfisher is a shy, beautiful bird of aquamarine and white with a long orange beak. Despite its English name it doesn't actually catch fish, but hunts in the forest, diving for insects from a low branch.

❀ *chibulubulu*. The Emerald-spotted Dove is a common bird in southern Africa. Its soft cooing can often be heard descending gently through the forest.

❀ *kadondwe cormorant*. The Reed Cormorant has a lovely long tail. It fishes in rivers, diving in one place, resurfacing elsewhere. Tonga children used to sing about these birds. A favourite game was to mimic their behaviour.

❀ *kampinumpinu grass*. A long grass with large seed heads. With sufficient skill, salt can be extracted from it.

❀ *luselo*. Bride price. In some cultures a man must pay a girl's family if he wants to marry her. She will be more expensive if she works hard and has been to school.

❀ *mopane trees*. These trees give good shade. When the sun is extremely hot the leaves fold to preserve moisture.

❉ *mululwe leaf.* Although this Winter Cassia tree smells nice, its leaves have a very bitter taste. When the fruit dries, it can be used as a comb.

❉ *munimbwa blossom.* The Tonga word literally means: the one who climbs. The *munimbwa* is a climbing jasmine whose flowers are noted for their great beauty.

❉ *musikili tree.* This tree of the mahogany family does not shed its leaves in the dry season. As well as providing good shade it is a useful source of food in time of famine. After boiling, the sweet seeds of the *musikili* can be eaten as a kind of porridge. The tree is also used in the preparation of a medicine or as an oil for the body.

❉ *musweezyo.* Although these green beans have a truly horrible taste they can be eaten when no other food is available. They are very difficult to find and must be peeled and then boiled for a long time. If they are not prepared correctly they are poisonous.

❉ *mutandamasenya tree.* If a sprig of this basil plant is placed on the fire then the fragrant smoke it produces will help to keep mosquitoes away. Doubly useful because not only are mosquitoes annoying but they also bring malaria, a disease that weakens and kills countless people in Africa. In southern Europe basil plants are placed on kitchen windowsills to keep flies away.

❉ *mutumu.* The bark of the cork bush, if prepared

correctly, can be used to make a drink.

❋ *muunga tree.* Often growing close to rivers, the buoyant wood of this acacia tree is frequently used for building canoes. It also provides such good shade from the hot sun that when land is cleared to grow crops *muunga* trees are left in the ground to shade those working in the fields. Its beans are eaten in time of want but, as with many famine foods, only after a meticulous preparation. They must first be soaked and cooked in their pods. Then, having been shelled, they must be cooked in water in which wood ash has been placed. After this the beans must then be soaked in some fresh water. Getting it wrong would make the eater ill, or even kill them.

❋ *nkulyukulyu starlings.* Like our own starlings, these red-winged starlings sleep together in tightly woven flocks, dispersing to feed during the day. Striking to look at, their body is a very dark blue, their wing tips an orange-red. They often chat and whistle from deep within the bush.

❋ *nsima.* A kind of porridge made from the crushed seeds of maize or millet. This is the staple food of many sub-Saharan people.

❋ *ntombo granary.* To protect the harvest from scavenging animals, such as rats or baboons, and any damaging moisture, it is kept in little huts built on stilts.

These granaries are very important parts of a village.

❊ *ntuntu*. This is an old Tonga custom where young people learnt about the tasks and responsibilities of marriage. It's a bit like children playing house together.

❊ *passop vir de hond*. 'Beware of the dog' in Afrikaans, a language spoken in South Africa.

❊ *qhapela inyoka*. 'Beware of the snake' in Zulu, a language spoke in South Africa.

❊ *quelea finches*. These little birds, also called *kashanga* by the Tonga, feed together in huge flocks. Drifting over the fields they looks like pillars of smoke. They can be very destructive, eating a village's entire crop in one day.

❊ *shebeen*. A place that serves alcohol without a licence. A sort of unofficial pub. The word *shebeen* is an Irish Gaelic word that has been adopted in southern Africa.

❊ *Sikatonga*. In the past Europeans might have used the term *witchdoctor* for a *Sikatonga*. Part priest, part doctor, the *Sikatonga* deals with the unexplained aspects of life, often using traditional medicine.

❊ *tsotsi*. A thief or a cheat.

❊ *yebo*. A widely used Zulu and Ndebele word in southern Africa. It can be a greeting or simply mean 'yes'.

❊ *windi*. The driver of a bus often employs someone to help him collect tickets and put the luggage on the roof of the bus. Buses can be very crowded and chaotic!

HISTORICAL NOTE

At the heart of the novel lies a historical injustice. Up until the 1950s many Tonga lived on the banks of the river Zambezi. When that river was dammed to make the mighty Lake Kariba, the people were simply moved from their rich lands. They found themselves in a strange and far less fertile environment. Lake Kariba powers a huge hydro-electric installation but the Tonga people themselves have never benefited from it, even though they made the ultimate sacrifice for its construction.

Acknowledgements: *The People of the Great River*,
Mike Tremmel and the River Tonga People,
Mambo Press in association with Silveira House.
Lwaano Lwanyika, Tonga book of the Earth,
Pamela Reynolds, Colleen Crawford, published
by Colleen Crawford in association with
Save the Children Fund (UK).

EGMONT PRESS: ETHICAL PUBLISHING

Egmont Press is about turning writers into successful authors and children into passionate readers – producing books that enrich and entertain. As a responsible children's publisher, we go even further, considering the world in which our consumers are growing up.

Safety First
Naturally, all of our books meet legal safety requirements. But we go further than this; every book with play value is tested to the highest standards – if it fails, it's back to the drawing-board.

Made Fairly
We are working to ensure that the workers involved in our supply chain – the people that make our books – are treated with fairness and respect.

Responsible Forestry
We are committed to ensuring all our papers come from environmentally and socially responsible forest sources.

For more information, please visit our website at
www.egmont.co.uk/ethicalpublishing